THE LOST ONES

A NOVEL

BOOK TWO
THE BOUNTY HUNTER

G. MICHAEL HOPF

For information contact:
geoff@gmichaelhopf.com
www.gmichaelhopf.com

ISBN-13: 978-1726225793
ISBN-10: 1726225798

DEDICATION

TO THOSE WHO GO MISSING AND ARE NEVER FOUND

"If the people we love are stolen from us, the way to have them live on is to never stop loving them."

—James O'Barr

PROLOGUE

TOPEKA, KANSAS

APRIL 4, 1891

Anna ran into the parlor to find her mother sitting comfortably in a wingback chair, casually crocheting. "Mama, can Emma and I go to the park?"

Clara looked at Anna with a broad smile then turned to check the time on the mantel clock. "I'm not sure. Supper will be on the table in an hour."

"Please, Mama," Anna whined.

Emma came in just behind Anna and cried out, "Please, Mama, please!"

Anna and Emma were fraternal twins, but their close resemblance had many people thinking they could be identical. The girls were tall for their age of fourteen. Standing over five feet five inches, they towered over their peers in school.

Clara frowned and sighed. "I need you to go help set the table—"

"If we set the table now, can we go?" Anna pressed.

Clara stared at their tender faces and relented. "Fine, but you must be back by five thirty. Supper will be served promptly."

"Yeah!" Emma sang out before bolting towards the dining room with Anna close behind.

The girls quickly set the table then exited the house,

slamming the door behind them. They sprinted down the sidewalk, passing the capitol building on their left, the dome sitting half constructed behind a tower of scaffolding.

Anna raced towards the park gleefully. Ever since the city had erected the swing set, she and Emma found themselves there daily. Entering the park, they found each seat on the swing set occupied. "Oh no."

Emma ran up and said, "Let's ask if they'll let us have a turn."

The girls walked up and asked each child, but none would give up their seat.

Disappointed but not about to surrender, they stood and stared at the other children.

A man approached, his shadow casting long over them, and asked, "You girls ever see a tiger? How about a lion?"

Anna turned to face the man. A shiver ran through her body when she laid her eyes upon the dark towering figure.

Emma cocked her head and answered him, "Only in books."

The man pointed towards a tree near the swings and said, "I'm with the circus."

The girls looked at the poster he was pointing towards. Anna read the headline out loud, "Great American Circus in Topeka, April 5 to 9."

"Oh, Anna, I've heard about this. We should have Mama and Pa take us," Emma squealed with joy.

"I strongly suggest you do, but how would you like

to get a preview of what's to be showcased?" the man asked with a toothy grin.

Skeptical, Anna replied, "I don't know, sir. We have to get back soon."

"It's just down at the riverfront. It'll only take a couple of minutes. You see, I'm in charge of the wild cats. I have a lion and tiger down there in a cage. You must see them; they're big and beautiful creatures, not as fearsome as they make out."

"I want to see," Emma chirped.

Anna took Emma by the arm and turned her. She looked at her deeply and said, "I don't think this is a good idea."

"Is it because you think I'm a stranger?"

"Of course, we don't know you," Anna replied.

"My name is Albert," he said, holding out his hand.

Emma took it and said, "My name is Emma, and that's my sister, Anna."

"Nice to meet you. Now see, we're not strangers anymore," he joked.

"I just don't think it's a good idea," Anna said.

"Young ladies, I don't have much time and I don't offer this to many people. If you don't wish to have this once-in-a-lifetime experience, I'll offer it to one of those children over there," he said, pointing to the swings. He waited for a response from them, but they stood, each looking at each other. "I bid you good day," he said, tipping his brown suede hat and stepping off.

"No..." Emma said loudly. She turned to Anna and snapped, "The gentleman is right; this is a once-in-a-lifetime experience. Let's go see the lion and tiger."

"Emma, I don't think so," Anna urged.

The man paused, but when he saw Anna wouldn't budge, he again walked off.

"Anna, stop being so…stubborn. This can be fun," Emma said and ran after Albert. "I'll go with you."

Albert looked at Emma then put his attention on Anna, who glared at him. "Your sister won't join you?"

Emma looked back at Anna and sneered, "No, she's a stick in the mud, as my pa would say."

"Oh, I wouldn't say that, she's just more cautious, and you have to be," he replied. He extended his arm and said, "Shall we?"

Emma took his arm.

The two began to walk north towards the riverfront.

Anna clenched her fists in anger, not with the man, but with Emma. There was no way she'd be able to go home and tell her parents that she'd just let her sister walk off with a strange man. Not wanting them to get out of sight, she cried out, "Wait up!"

Albert and Emma stopped and looked back.

Anna ran up to them and said, "I'm coming too."

Albert smiled and said, "I promise you this will be a truly magnificent experience, something you'll be able to tell your children."

"I'm glad you're coming," Emma said.

"You didn't give me a choice," Anna growled under her breath.

"This will be fun. Stop being a fuddy-duddy," Emma jabbed.

"We can't be long; we need to see them then run home. Remember, we need to be back in time for supper or Mama will be angry with us," Anna warned.

"I promise it won't take long," Albert said.

A strong and cool wind swept in from the north, giving Anna a chill. She then wondered if that odd and unexpected current of air was portending what lay ahead. She couldn't shake the anxious feeling that sat in her gut. Something kept nagging at her not to trust this man.

The three walked the six blocks to the riverfront. Along the banks of the river to the right, a narrow dock serviced a warehouse; moored to the dock sat an old timbered barge with a large cabin.

Anna looked at it then to her left; there she saw only a vacant lot with tall grasses. "Where's the lion and tiger?"

"Just on that barge there," Albert said, nudging them towards the dock.

"Where?" Anna asked again, standing her ground and not moving an inch closer.

"In the cabin," Albert said.

Thrilled to go see, Emma headed towards the barge without question.

"Emma, stop. This doesn't feel right," Anna called out.

"Come on, Anna," Emma called out, waving her arm.

Albert turned to Anna and said, "Aren't you going to come?"

"No, I don't believe you," she replied. "Emma, don't step foot on that barge. It's time to go home."

Emma didn't listen; she kept pressing forward.

Anna felt a sickening feeling overcome her. The hairs on the back of her neck rose as she felt a presence behind her. She turned and saw two men coming up quickly. She gasped, turning back to cry out to Emma, only to find that another man had grabbed her. "Wait, no!"

Albert walked up to her and said, "Be quiet or we'll kill your sister."

"Emma, no!" Anna wailed.

The two men behind her snatched her forcibly, each grabbing an arm.

Anna tried to resist, but the men were too strong.

Albert approached her and warned, "You cry out one more time, I promise you'll regret it."

"I hate you," Anna said. "You're a liar."

Albert put his hand over her mouth and pressed down hard. "You shut that trap of yours if you know what's best for you." He looked up and down the street from where they came to make sure no one had heard or seen them. He gave one of the men holding Anna a nod and ordered, "Take her to the barge with the other one and tie them up."

Anna kicked and hollered, "Help."

Albert pulled a bandana from his pocket and shoved it into her mouth. "That will keep you quiet."

The two men picked her up and ran towards the barge.

With each step closer to the barge, Anna's terror increased. Her eyes darted back and forth with hopes a stranger or passerby would see what was happening and come save them, but none appeared. When they took her onto the barge, her heart dropped, as she knew once she was placed in the cabin, she'd be gone for good, never again to see Topeka, her parents, nothing she was familiar with. Why had she allowed this to happen? She knew from the start the man was no good and meant them harm, yet she allowed Emma to go with him and further allowed herself to be abducted. She had failed, and this failure could very well be her last.

CHAPTER ONE

WICHITA, KANSAS

APRIL 7, 1891

Abigail sighed loudly when she looked at her reflection in the mirror. "No, never, no!"

Her partner, Dwight, laughed. "Abby, you and I know this is the only way to get him."

She turned around and barked, "I haven't worn a dress in…I don't know, in a long time, and this…this doesn't even count as a dress. This is just degrading," she said of the tightly fitted corset top.

"I think you look…um, how do I say it?" Dwight asked rhetorically.

"You say it, you get a slug in ya," she snapped. She liked Dwight, but at the moment, she was having a tough time dealing with the arrangement she had agreed to in order to get a bounty they'd been chasing for a few weeks. Dwight had been her partner for over a year and the one person she had come to trust since becoming a bounty hunter after her first job with Grant Toomey back in Miles City, Montana. Thoughts of her first job came to her often. She missed Grant and was thankful for what knowledge he had bestowed on her in their brief time together.

"I know this isn't an ideal situation, but you agreed

to do this," Dwight said, rocking back in his chair, his hands in his lap and a broad smile on his chiseled face.

"There has to be another way," she grunted as she sat in a chair opposite him.

"You look very uncomfortable, but we can't get close to him, you know that. Every time we've tried, he seems to be one step ahead of us. He only seems to let his guard down around women dressed like that," Dwight said, pointing at her.

She looked down at her outfit and said, "I don't think this is worth three hundred dollars."

"It is, and catching Ted will bring us more clout," Dwight said.

"Can't we just shoot him in the leg or something?" she asked, knowing the answer already.

"I wish we could, but he's wanted alive…period. Believe me, if it were a matter of dead or alive, we'd have killed him outside Olathe."

She sighed as she picked at the puffy skirt and skintight leggings. "Why does my life have to be this difficult?"

"Abby, this job is good for us. It will cement us as a solid bounty-hunting team."

"I know, I know," she lamented.

"Shall we run through it all again?" Dwight asked concerning the plan.

"Sure," she said.

"With the help of Eloise, we can get you into the brothel. Ted has been visiting every night this week, and each time he asks for a new girl, a young girl. Fortunately, you're young and look even younger; that's the way he likes them," Dwight said.

"I know we can't kill him, but can I bash his face in?" Abby asked.

"Yes, you can. Now let me get back to the plan," he said, smiling. "Eloise has agreed that she will take Ted to the room you're in. Once he's in there with you, get him undressed—"

Interrupting Dwight, Abby said, "Can I shoot him? In the knee or something?"

"No, we can't afford to have him die of blood loss or infection. Now be quiet and let me finish," Dwight said, frowning.

"Go ahead."

"It's best if you can get him undressed, which will leave him unarmed. When he is, simply knock on the wall that the head of the bed is against; I'll be in the next room. I'll come right in; we'll subdue him and haul him off to the marshal's office, collect the bounty, and head to the next job."

"I'm warning you, if he touches me, I can't guarantee I won't stab him or something," Abby warned.

Dwight leaned in and said, "Abby, we've been working together awhile now. I need you to promise me you won't mess this job up. We've spent too long for this to go south tonight. Promise me."

"I can't, you know I can't," she said.

"Promise me," he said more sternly.

She looked away, deliberately ignoring his request.

"Abby!"

"Yes, I promise," she shot back, annoyed by his pleas.

"Good, after tonight we'll go celebrate over a root beer and whiskey," Dwight said.

Abby had stuck to her principles of not drinking alcohol. After seeing what it had done to her father, she pledged to never touch a drop, and so far she'd been successful. When she did go out, she'd partake in a couple of cool root beers or even a sarsaparilla.

"You're buying," she snarled.

"Drinks are on me, you have my word," Dwight said. Looking past her, he saw an open letter on the vanity. "Is that from Madeleine?"

Madeleine was a sore subject for her and not one she wished to discuss just before executing a job. "Let's talk about tonight."

"So she wrote you?" he asked.

"I don't want to talk about it," she replied.

"Are you going to write her back?" he asked, still pressing.

"No, I'm not. I told you what happened; now leave it at that," she growled.

"There's a little girl in Texas that misses you. You have to write back," he said.

Folding her arms, she barked, "I'm not going to say it again, I'm not going to talk about it."

Unrelenting, he continued, "I think there's a correlation between the ill temper you show so often now and you leaving Madeleine the way you did last time you saw her."

Fuming, she snapped, "Do you like to prod me? Do you?"

Seeing her anger rise to a level that she was probably about to burst, he sat quietly pledging to himself not to say another word about Madeleine.

She paced the room a couple of times and asked, "Say, how did you convince Eloise to let us into her brothel?" She was genuinely curious about how Dwight had managed to secure a deal with the hardnosed owner of the most popular brothel in town.

He leaned back in his chair with a devilish grin and said, "I have my ways."

Raising her hand, Abby said, "Enough, I don't need to hear another utterance from you."

"Are you sure? I can give you the details," Dwight joked.

She leapt to her feet, looked out the window, and noticed the sun had just set below the horizon. She walked over to a small table in the corner and picked up her Colt. She half-cocked the hammer and spun the cylinder, not for any reason but to hear the sound; it had become a habit of hers. Using her thumb, she slowly lowered the hammer back, lifted her skirt, and slid the pistol into a holster she had strapped around her upper thigh. Catching a glimpse of herself in the mirror, she cocked her head and practiced a seductive look.

"What are you doing?" he asked.

"Preparing," she replied.

"Good, glad to see you're taking this seriously," he said.

She spun around, pointed at her outfit and snarked, "I always take jobs seriously; I just happen not to like the particulars of this is all. So, if you're done sitting around feeling proud of yourself, how about we go catch Ted."

"That's the Abby I know," he said, springing to his feet.

Seeing his enthusiasm, her stern composure melted away. A big smile stretched across her face and she said, "It's time to go collect that bounty."

***

Abigail anxiously waited for Eloise to bring Ted to her. Each job she took always came with pitfalls and potential obstacles, but this one had proven to be very challenging. Dwight was right; if they could get the elusive Ted McKnight, they'd score not only the bounty but would add to their growing reputation. Abigail was more nervous than usual. She hadn't taken a job that required the target to be taken alive. She and Dwight had only come across jobs that gave them the option, and falling back on Grant's advice from years ago, it was better and easier to just kill the target than nab them alive. The risks were always higher, and this had proven the toughest in her few years of collecting bounties.

As she waited for the eventual knock on the door, she paced the small room. Several times she practiced lifting her skirt and pulling out her pistol. Without Dwight's knowledge, she had also hidden knives in the room.

A tap on the door pulled her away from her thoughts. "Yes," she called out, a tinge of anxiety trembling across her vocal cords.

"It's Minnie. I have some hot water for the bath." Minnie was a young disabled girl who worked for Eloise at the brothel.

"It's open," Abigail said.

The door swung open and in came Minnie, limping as she took each step. In her arms she cradled a bucket of steaming water. She hobbled to the steel claw-foot tub and dumped the water in. Right behind her came two other women; they too were carrying pails of hot water. Like Minnie, they dumped the water and promptly exited.

"We'll come back with more," Minnie said, a gentle smile on her face.

"Is he here?" Abigail asked.

"Yes, downstairs getting liquored up. Eloise has informed him you're up here. I suspect he will come up soon," Minnie answered.

Curious, Abigail asked, "The other girls, what have they said about him?"

"You don't know?" Minnie replied.

"I wouldn't ask if I knew the answer."

"He likes a new girl each time 'cause he tends to get a bit rough," Minnie said, stepping out of the room, closing the door behind her.

This was information that Dwight had either left out or decided to keep from her. Unnerved, Abigail went and checked the three knives she had hidden around the room. One under the mattress, the hilt sticking out just enough for her to grab; one in the top drawer of a small side table; and the last one under a stack of towels next to the tub.

She wanted the bounty, but she wouldn't allow him to beat her. After a childhood of beatings from her alcoholic father, she swore to never let anyone touch her in an aggressive manner, nor would she be witness to the abuse of a child.

The door opened, to her surprise. It was Minnie and the other two women; they carried in the buckets and dumped them in the tub. The two unknown women left the room without uttering a word, leaving Minnie and Abigail.

"How badly did he beat the others?" Abigail asked Minnie.

"Enough that we had to call the doc. He likes his women battered, bloody and unable to resist," Minnie said soberly.

Abigail clenched her jaw and thought about what to say next.

"I best be going. He will be up here soon, and if he sees me in here, he'll swat me," Minnie said.

"He's hit you too?" Abigail asked.

Minnie lifted her hair from her neck and turned towards Abigail. "He did this the first night he was here. Said I interrupted him."

Anger welled up inside Abigail. The temptation to just strike Ted down the second she saw him rose in her.

"You must really need the money," Minnie said.

"What does he like to do when he first comes into

the room? Take a bath?" Abigail asked.

"No, that's for after. He prefers to defile women while he's filthy," Minnie answered. "I have to leave. I'll be just down the hall after he's done. I'll clean you up afterwards." Minnie swiftly turned and exited the room.

Abigail walked over and closed the door. She and Dwight had suspected the bath he wanted was for before, not after. This changed things. This meant he would enter the room and begin beating and raping. The plan needed to change and now. Abigail briskly walked towards the wall so she could signal Dwight.

The door of the room flew open and there stood Ted. He was a towering and menacing figure, standing over six foot six, with wide muscular shoulders and massive arms that hung long. He saw Abigail and grinned. "Aren't you a pretty little thing," he said, stepping into the room and blocking her way to the far wall.

Abigail instantly fell out of her role and snapped, "Don't you dare touch me."

Ted slammed the door shut and laughed. "Eloise got me one who wants to resist. I love it."

Abigail backed up towards the tub, stopping when the backs of her legs touched the edge.

Ted tossed his hat onto a chair, removed his gun belt and slung it on the rear bedpost. He unbuckled the belt that held his pants and pulled it out fast. He bent it in half and slapped it against the palm of his hand. "Someone needs a whippin'."

Abigail thought about drawing her gun but hesitated. She had gotten this far in life dealing with brutes like him;

plus she really wanted that bounty.

Ted took a couple of steps towards her, but by his approach he was merely toying with her to get a reaction.

"You hit me with that, I'll…" Abigail warned, pointing at the belt.

"You'll what?" Ted chuckled.

"I'll take it from you and whip you with it," Abigail blurted out, only realizing how stupid it sounded after she said it.

"Whip me? Ha, you really like to play, don't you?" Ted said, taking another step towards her.

In the corner of her eye, she spotted the stack of towels to her left.

"I don't want you to play nice," Ted said and again took a step.

He was now four feet away from her. His immense stature in the small room made him seem even larger than he was.

Abigail had never fought a man this size without her Colt in her grip. She knew she couldn't match his strength or his size, so she'd have to outwit him. "You're right, I won't play nice, but you'll have to catch me first."

Ted straightened his spine, cocked his head enough to make it crack, and without saying a word, launched himself towards her.

Using her quick reflexes, Abigail dodged his advance, went to reach under the towels, but missed the knife.

The inertia from Ted's lunge landed him in the tub. Wet and angry, he stood tall and cried out, "Come here!"

Abigail leapt across the bed, opened the drawer of

the nightstand, and pulled the four-inch knife out. She turned, but Ted was on top of her. He wrapped his trunk-like arms around her in a bear hug and slammed her into the mattress. The force from the throw caused her to drop the knife on the floor.

Ted looked down at it and growled, "A knife? You were going to stab me?" He forcibly grabbed her arm and squeezed hard.

Abigail tried to pull away, but his grip was too hard. With her left arm being held by Ted, she clenched her right hand into a fist, cocked it back, and threw a punch. Her fist slammed into Ted's nose.

The blow to his face didn't stun him at all. His eyes widened, and in a fit of anger, he cocked back and threw his own punch. He struck Abigail in the side of the head. The hit was enough to stun her and give Ted the advantage he needed. He jumped on top of her, straddling his legs around her small torso and pinning her arms to the bed. "Now you'll do what I want you to do."

Abigail looked around and noticed she was seeing double. Ted had delivered a heavy blow to her head, one she'd never experienced before. She mumbled something unintelligible under her breath.

Unable to make out what she said, he asked, "What was that?"

She mumbled again.

He leaned down and asked, "Are you begging? Huh? I want you to beg." He leaned down to listen.

With the side of his face inches from hers, she saw an opportunity and lashed out. She clamped her teeth down on his left ear and twisted her head back and forth.

Ted howled in pain and pulled away, only to leave a chunk of his ear in her mouth. "Argh!" He jumped off her, holding his ear as blood poured freely from the wound.

Abigail spit out the bloody chunk and gave him a devilish smile.

"I'll kill you for that," Ted screamed.

She wasn't going to allow that to happen. She rolled off the opposite side of the bed, reached down, pulled her skirt up, and removed her Colt. She cocked the hammer and leveled the muzzle at him. "You won't be killing me or anyone else anymore, Ted McKnight. You're coming with me."

He gave her an odd look and said, "You think you're taking me in?"

"Yes."

He put his right hand down to where his pistol would normally hang from his hip and found it wasn't there. He then caught sight of it hanging on the bedpost.

"Give it up. You're coming with me," Abigail said.

"You're not going to shoot me. I'm wanted alive, and you won't take the chance on killing me," Ted boasted, his left hand still holding what was left of his ear.

"It doesn't say I can't shoot you in the kneecap," Abigail said. She pointed the pistol at his right knee and squeezed the trigger. The .45-caliber round exploded from the muzzle and tore through the front of his kneecap and burst out the back.

Ted's right leg buckled and gave out. He dropped to

the floor and cried out in pain. "You shot me!"

Feeling stronger than ever, Abigail walked over to Ted and said, "Ted McKnight, I'm Abby Sure Shot, and you're now my prisoner." She swung her right hand back then came down on top of Ted's head with the butt of her pistol grip.

Ted's eyes rolled back into his head. He fell backwards onto the hardwood floor with a thud.

Abigail stepped forward and looked down.

The door burst open. Dwight came rushing in, his pistol drawn. He looked at Abigail first then saw the blood. His eyes traced it back to Ted lying unconscious on the floor. "Please tell me you didn't kill him."

"He's alive, but that son of a bitch deserves to die a slow death," Abigail said.

"I heard a gunshot," Dwight said.

"'Cause I shot him in the knee. We don't need him running off," Abigail answered.

"But we can't risk—"

Interrupting him, Abigail snapped, "You weren't here to know what happened, but it wasn't looking good two minutes ago."

Dwight suddenly noticed the side of Abigail's face. He approached her and asked, "Are you okay?"

She turned away from him and said, "We need to tie him up."

"Did he hit you?" Dwight asked, his voice indicating concern.

"Go get some rope; then pull the wagon up front so we can deliver him to the marshal's office in Olathe right away."

"But are you okay?" Dwight again asked.

"I'll be fine. Now go get me some rope," she barked.

Dwight raced out of the room.

Abigail stepped closer to Ted and knelt down. She could smell the alcohol coming from his pores. It immediately brought her back to her childhood and her father. Repulsed, she looked away from Ted and stood back up. In the open doorway she caught sight of Minnie lingering. "Everything is fine."

Minnie stepped out of the shadows and peered down at Ted. "How did you stop him?"

Abigail nodded at her pistol and said, "With this." Then using her left index finger, she pointed at her head and continued, "And with this."

SPRINGFIELD, MISSOURI

Today was the day that Gavin was going to tell his parents about his plans. He was turning eighteen tomorrow, so according to the law and by all rights, he was an adult, so therefore able to make his own decisions. He had spent his entire day in the fields, going over and over how he'd break the news to them that he was moving to Jefferson City and taking an apprenticeship at a printing house. He wasn't quite sure how'd they take the news, but if he was to follow his dreams, he had to do it, because he hoped to learn the trade and maybe one day own a printing company. He loved reading and devoured books and newspapers anytime he could get his hands on them, but he'd tried his hand at writing, and he just didn't have it. Working for a printer would get him as close to making books as he'd get without being an author.

His mother, Matilda, placed freshly baked bread on the table and took a seat. "Father, want to lead us in prayer?" she asked Langdon, her husband.

Langdon was a tall and lean man, towering over six feet three inches, with long slender arms and legs. His hair was thick and black, but the most prominent feature on him was his large crooked nose; Matilda would often describe it as distinguished.

Gavin didn't get his father's genes; in fact, if Langdon hadn't been there for his birth, he would have questioned whether he was related to either one of them. He was short, standing only about five feet six, had dirty blond hair, and even his nose was the opposite of his father's, as it was long and slender. Matilda said he was the spitting image of her grandfather, who had died young in life while working as a fisherman.

Langdon nodded and said, "Yes, Mother, I'll say the blessing."

"Excuse me, but could I say the blessing?" Gavin asked, to his parents' surprise.

"If your father doesn't mind, why not? It will be the last time you say it before you become a man," she said.

Langdon nodded his approval.

Gavin recited their nightly blessing, and when he was done, he said, "I have an announcement."

"You do? Please tell us, dear," Matilda said, passing a bowl of mashed potatoes to Langdon, who was piling food on his plate and seemed unconcerned about what Gavin had to say.

"As you said, Mother, I turn eighteen tomorrow and I'll officially be a man; well, as my first act as a man, I will be moving to Jefferson City and taking an apprenticeship with the Clancy Printing House."

"Oh my," Matilda said, dropping her fork.

Langdon stopped chewing, set his silverware down, and slowly turned his head until his eyes were locked on Gavin. "You're leaving the farm?"

"Yes, Father, I'm leaving. I have a passion and I want to follow it. You know how much I enjoy books and, well, this is the only way I can get close to them without actually being a writer."

"Son, I'll need you for the harvest come the end of summer," Langdon said.

"You said just last month that we did very well last season and that you were looking at acquiring some additional land, but you held back; so you have the money to hire someone," Gavin said.

"Sweetheart, Jefferson City is very far away. How will you get there, and where will you live?" Matilda asked.

"I corresponded with the general manager, a Mr. Fitzpatrick, and they will reimburse me for the coach, and they have lodgings on site for all apprentices as well as three meals a day provided, and they even offer an ale each evening," Gavin said with a smile, as he was looking forward to drinking beer.

"I don't feel well," Matilda said, placing her head in her hand.

"I need you. Can't you wait until after the harvest? How about next year, say January?" Langdon asked.

"Father, this apprenticeship is hard to get, and they want me. I had to write an essay to get it, and they were so impressed. If I do well, I'll probably be moved up to typesetting by this time next year," Gavin said.

"Where am I going to find someone to replace you this quickly?" Langdon asked, his tone shifting from shock to annoyance.

"There's plenty of day laborers in town. I'm sure you can find someone who will be dependable. They can even live above the barn in that space," Gavin answered. It was clear he'd thought through all the possible questions because his answers were coming fast.

"I don't think you can go so quickly, Gavin; let's talk more about this over the summer, and maybe we can get you an apprenticeship in the fall. I could possibly do that," Langdon said.

"Father, you don't understand. This position won't be open then," Gavin countered.

"You don't know that," Langdon said.

"You're right, I don't know. What I do know is its available now and they want me. If I let this go, I may never get this opportunity again," Gavin said.

"Son, I'm sorry, but you don't have my blessing to go. You might be turning eighteen, but you're a young eighteen, not ready for the real world. Now, let's stop talking about this and eat while the food is still warm," Langdon said, stabbing a piece of roast.

"I don't need your blessing. I'll be eighteen and I'll

be a man. I can make my own decisions!" Gavin snapped.

Langdon's eyes widened with anger. "Did you just raise your voice to me?"

"Yes, Father, I did. I'm not a boy anymore, I'm a man, and this is what I want to do," Gavin said, standing up from the table and tossing his napkin onto his plate.

Langdon slammed his fist down and barked, "Sit down now!"

"No!" Gavin barked back.

"You're not eighteen yet, so you're still young enough for a whippin'!" Langdon said, getting to his feet and reaching for Gavin, who evaded his grasp.

"Langdon, Gavin, both of you, just stop this!" Matilda hollered.

"You come here, boy!" Langdon bellowed. He was normally a mild-mannered man who rarely raised his voice, nor had he ever physically punished Gavin over the years, but tonight, he was making an exception.

Gavin backed away from the table and said, "No, Father, I won't have you put your hands on me."

Langdon's anger was quickly turning to rage.

Seeing this, Matilda jumped up and got in front of Langdon. "Husband, you need to calm yourself. There is a way to solve this without punishing the boy. It will only cause him to leave."

Langdon took Matilda by the arms and moved her out of the way without harming her. "He needs to learn respect. I thought he was a good child until tonight."

"Don't come near me, Father," Gavin said.

"No, son, you need to understand one fundamental

fact about life. You don't get to say or do what you please when you're not the one in charge," Langdon said as he marched towards Gavin.

Gavin backed himself into a corner and began to shudder. He'd never seen his father so angry and didn't know what to do about it.

Langdon grabbed Gavin and pushed him against the table, knocking a couple of cups over. He removed his belt and began to whip Gavin with it, each swing striking him in the buttocks.

Gavin wailed in pain.

"Langdon, stop it this instant!" Matilda screamed.

"Not until I whip his insubordination out of him," Langdon replied, taking another swipe at Gavin.

Unable to watch anymore, Matilda grabbed Langdon's arm when it was recoiled back and held it with all her strength. "Stop it, now!"

Langdon looked at her, wild-eyed, and saw pain and sorrow in her eyes. He lowered his arm and tossed the belt aside. "The boy will not treat me this way. I don't know what's gotten into him. Maybe he read it somewhere."

With Langdon calmed down, Matilda checked on Gavin, who was weeping. As she petted his head, she asked, "Are you okay?"

Gavin's shock quickly turned to anger. He stood up straight, gave her a hard stare and replied, "I'm not okay, Mother, not at all." He shrugged her embrace off and bolted for his room.

"Gavin, come back. Let's talk about this," Matilda

pleaded.

"Let him be. He needs to think about his actions and his absurd plan. It's not happening; the boy is not leaving. He can't; we need him. We've given him everything his whole life, and this is how he repays us, by leaving when it's the most inconvenient?"

"He'll be eighteen tomorrow, and I seem to recall you up and left your father when you turned eighteen," Matilda reminded him.

"My father was a drunk, a no-good man who didn't provide. I left so I could make money for the family. How about getting the story correct? And Gavin is so innocent. I fear he won't do well out there," he snapped.

Matilda approached him and placed her small hands on his heaving chest. "He's been a good son, a loving son. He wishes to better his life, that's all. I hear your point about him and, yes, he's naïve, but that makes him special."

"A better life? So working for a printer is better than being a farmer?" Langdon asked.

"For him it is," she said.

"I need him in those fields tomorrow and the day after, the week after," Langdon said.

Lowering her voice even more, she said in a soothing tone, "We have the money; we can both hire and acquire more land. Let's do that. We don't need a new wagon, and I don't need a new dress."

"But you need a new dress, you've been denying yourself something like that for a while, and I want to give it to you."

"We'll make do, we always have. Now go in there and talk to him nicely," she said, nudging him towards Gavin's bedroom door.

Her appeal to calm worked. "It's best we sleep on this. Maybe he'll change his mind," Langdon said, relenting to allow whatever would happen to happen.

"We don't go to bed angry in this household. Go talk to your son," she said, this time pushing his hulking body a few steps closer to the door.

"I'll go," he said, raising his arms as if he were surrendering. He walked to the door and knocked. "Gavin, son, open the door."

Silence.

Langdon tapped louder. "Gavin, open up. I want to discuss what just happened and tell you I'm sorry."

No reply.

Langdon looked over his shoulder at Matilda and shrugged his shoulders.

"Just open the door. He's probably too upset to answer you," she said.

Langdon turned the latch and pushed the door open wide. A gush of cool evening air hit him. He looked and saw the window was open. Glancing around the small room, he saw that Gavin wasn't there. Turning towards Matilda, he said, "He's gone."

"What? No," she said, running to the front door and throwing it open. Out onto the front porch she ran. "Gavin, come back."

"Maybe he went to the barn," Langdon said, pushing past her, a lantern in his hand.

"Gavin, where are you?" she cried out.

Langdon ran off the porch and towards the barn. "Gavin, son, are you in there?" He tossed open the barn door and looked inside but found nothing but equipment and hay for the two cows. "Gavin!"

Matilda sprinted farther out near the lane and hollered, "Gavin, don't leave us. Please come back!"

Gavin heard their cries from a distance but didn't stop to look back. He'd keep going until he reached his final destination, Jefferson City.

CHAPTER TWO

OLATHE, KANSAS

APRIL 8, 1891

Marshal Stevens shook his head in disbelief. "How did you get him?"

"Skills, cunning and—" Dwight said but was interrupted.

"Me," Abigail said.

"And she took a hit or two from the big guy," Dwight said.

"You got him by yourself?" Steven asked, his gaze still fixed on Ted sitting in one of his jail cells. "We've been trying to get him for some time." He looked at Abigail's face and continued, "And you came away still looking good."

"I have a good bruise on my left arm, and my head still hurts, but I'll live," Abigail said proudly.

"But in the end, it was all a team effort," Dwight said, giving Abigail a stare.

The front door of the marshal's office opened. The light of the late afternoon came sweeping in along with a short man cradling a camera in his arms.

"Who are you, and what do you want?" Stevens barked at the man.

The man put the camera down, closed the door,

removed his bowler hat, and nodded. "Barret Fisk at your service. I'm with the *Kansas City Star.* I was in town following another story when I heard Ted McKnight had been brought in by the famous Abby Sure Shot."

Stevens gave Abigail a look and asked, "You're Abby Sure Shot?"

Abigail's face turned flush.

"She is and I'm Dwight—"

Stevens pushed past Dwight and stuck his hand out. "It's a pleasure to meet you. I've heard a lot about your exploits and that you even rode with Hammer Tillis."

Abigail reluctantly shook Stevens' hand and said, "I did. He was a good man."

"Good? He was a stone-faced killer," Steven said.

Abigail pulled her hand back from him and said, "When can we collect the bounty?"

"I can have that transferred to the bank you mentioned when you arrived in town a few weeks back. Will that do?" Stevens asked.

"That'll be fine," Abigail replied. With few options for collecting bounties back then, Abigail and Dwight typically went for the banking deposit. If they wanted the cash they'd have to wait around and that was something Abigail loathed to do.

Fisk approached and, like Stevens, stuck his hand out to Abigail. "Miss Sure Shot, is it okay if I call you that?"

"Abby is fine," Abigail said.

Dwight stood watching the interactions with a look of irritation on his face.

"As soon as I heard you were in town, I had to come

meet you. Is it possible to get a photograph with you and Ted McKnight?"

"Oh, um, I'm not sure," Abigail said, looking at Dwight then back to Fisk.

"Of course it's fine. We'd love to," Dwight said.

"Ahh, who are you?" Fisk asked, looking at Dwight.

"I'm Dwight Daniels, her partner," Dwight answered.

"Oh, never heard of you; um, if you could go next to the cell over there and stand, I'll get a photograph," Fisk said, ignoring Dwight.

"Sure," Abigail said.

Fisk grabbed his equipment and began to set it up. This gave Dwight and Abigail time to chat.

"Before you blow your top, I can't help it if they don't know who you are," Abigail said to Dwight, sensing he was upset that no one seemed to know or care about him.

"I just expect you to correct people when they're wrong. Can you do that?" Dwight asked.

"I'm ready," Fisk said from behind his camera. In his right hand he held a tray with flash powder.

Abigail took up a position next to the bars with Dwight opposite her, leaving enough space in between to see Ted sitting in the cell beyond.

"Okay, and on the count of five," Fisk said. He slowly counted to five and removed the lens cover. The flash powder lit and popped; then he covered the lens again. "Got it. Now can I get a photograph with just Abby?"

"No, that was enough," Abigail said.

"Please, Miss Sure Shot."

"I said no," Abigail said.

"Very well, thank you," Fisk said.

Dwight looked at the clock on the wall and said, "Shall we check in and go get those drinks we promised ourselves?"

"Sure," Abigail said with a smile.

"I'd suggest the Olathe Inn down the street. Nice rooms and they have a good dining hall too," Stevens suggested.

"We'll do that," Dwight said, heading towards the door with Abigail following.

Outside, they found Olathe a quiet little town. It had charm, more so than other towns they'd recently visited. They stepped off and untied their horses. Just as they mounted, the door to the marshal's office opened and out came Fisk.

"Miss Sure Shot, do you have a moment to spare?" Fisk asked.

Settling into her saddle, Abigail replied, "Depends on how much you're asking for."

Fisk walked up to her and said, "I've been following your exploits for some time, and I have an interest in doing a full exposé on you. It might even turn into a book."

"What does that mean, exposé?" she asked.

"Many of the readers of the *Kansas City Star* would be interested in getting to know who you are, where you came from, and so forth and so on. What I'm proposing is…" Fisk said then stopped himself. He gave Dwight a look and realized he couldn't just sell Abigail, he'd also have to sell him. "How about I buy you both dinner?"

"If it includes drinks too, then yes," Dwight said.

Abigail scowled at Dwight and said to Fisk, "What do you want?"

"I want to write about you and your partner. I want to know how you captured Ted McKnight and all those others you've captured or killed. To be honest, I want to know everything; my readers want to know everything."

"Meet us in an hour at the dining hall. Supper is on you," Dwight said.

"I'm not so sure," Abigail said.

"Abby, we knew capturing Ted would bring us exposure, and this is it. We should do this, and if nothing comes of it, we got a free meal and drinks out of it," Dwight said.

Abigail thought for a second then gave her reply. "Meet us in an hour. We'll talk then."

"Great, thank you so much. You won't regret it," Fisk said excitedly.

TOPEKA, KANSAS

Edward Fulton, Anna and Emma's father, paced his ornately decorated study, a cold sweat stuck to his brow. His mind kept filling with the worst sorts of images of what could be happening to his beloved daughters. He imagined them begging, calling for him to come save them, but he was helpless, a position he rarely found himself in.

Edward was a highly successful businessman. His latest venture had been railroads, in which he'd found great fortune. He questioned if it was his very success that had made Anna and Emma targets for kidnapping and ransom, yet neither he nor the Topeka Police had received a communication from the kidnappers demanding a ransom. And if it wasn't kidnapping for ransom, what was it? Had they been abducted and killed already? Were they being tortured, raped even? Each time he considered the latter, his body shook with anger. For all his wealth and power, he was unable to do anything. He had employed the local police, and due to his previous generous donations, they came immediately upon hearing. However, they didn't have a witness nor a shred of evidence to lead them anywhere. Unwilling to sit and wait, he promptly placed a telegram to the Pinkerton Detective Agency in Chicago. Soon, two agents would be arriving in Topeka on a train so they could begin working on the case. Even with them coming, he wanted to do more; he needed to do more.

"Edward, please stop pacing. You're making me anxious," Clara said from a chaise lounge, a handkerchief clenched in her small hands.

Edward stopped and glared at her. "I'm sorry if how I think upsets you!"

"You're just making me…oh, what do I care," she said, getting to her feet and rushing towards the door.

"Clara, stop," Edward called out.

She halted at the doorway but didn't turn to face him.

"I will find them, I swear to you," he said.

"It's my fault," she cried.

He went to her side and wrapped his arms around her. "It's not your fault. You need to stop blaming yourself."

"I shouldn't have let them go. It was so close to supper, yet I knew how much they enjoyed the new park," Clara cried.

"If it's anyone's fault, it's mine for funding that park," Edward said.

"Will we ever find them?" Clara moaned.

"We will, I just know we will," Edward assured her.

She turned around to face him, her swollen brown eyes looking deeply into his. "Promise me."

"I promise," he replied, wiping the tears from her cheeks.

Feeling exhausted, she laid her head against his chest and began to sob.

He pulled her closer and kissed the top of her head. "I'll do whatever it takes. I'll hire whomever I need to. I'll never stop looking for them."

OUTSKIRTS OF KANSAS CITY, MISSOURI

Anna didn't know what was coming but knew something was about to happen after one of her captors came into the cabin and placed hoods over her and Emma.

The smell from the moldy canvas sack made her

nauseous, but she couldn't succumb to illness now. If there was going to be an opportunity to escape, it would be now.

From the commotion and chatter on the deck of the barge, it sounded as if they had just moored somewhere.

"What's happening?" Emma whimpered.

"I think we're being removed from the barge," Anna answered calmly.

"I'm scared," Emma said.

"Emma, I need you to do whatever I say, okay?" Anna said.

"Are they going to hurt us?" Emma asked.

"Yes, this is why we need to escape if we can," Anna said.

"But we're tied up, my arms are behind my back, and I can't see with this bag on my head," Emma cried.

"Are your legs tied?"

"No."

"Neither are mine. That means we can run."

"Run? Where? I can't even see," Emma complained.

"Just do what I say, when I say," Anna ordered.

A man stepped into the cabin and took Emma by the arm and lifted her. "You too, get up," he ordered Anna.

Anna stumbled but eventually got to her feet.

The man took Anna by the arm too and brought them onto the deck.

The afternoon sun had just set to the west, and soon they'd be enveloped by darkness.

"One hundred and twenty-five each, that was the price agreed to," Albert said to a group of men on the dock.

Hearing they were being sold, Anna knew they had to flee, but where? Unable to see, any attempt now would be fruitless and dangerous; but if she did nothing, she was guaranteed to be sold and possibly lost forever.

"Before we pay you, let me see them," a man said, stepping forward. He was short and rotund; his large belly hung over the waistband of his trousers.

"It's Samuel, right?" Albert asked the man.

"Yes, I'm the one paying you," Samuel replied.

"Show me the money and I'll show you the girls," Albert said.

Samuel turned around and nodded to one of his men, who promptly tossed a sack of coins to Samuel. "Look inside," Samuel said, opening the small sack and showing it to Albert.

Albert peeked inside, smiled and said, "Of course you can look at them." Albert nodded towards one of his men, who quickly snatched the hoods off both girls.

Now able to see, Anna began to calculate the decision to make a run for it. Unfortunately for them, they were on a makeshift dock, and the one thing standing in between them and land was Albert, Samuel and an entourage of others at the end of the dock.

"Thoughts?" Albert asked.

"They're pretty," Samuel said, taking Emma's face firmly in his grip and turning her head to get a better look.

Emma started to sob.

"Don't cry, girl. Soon you'll be in good hands,"

Samuel said, removing a handkerchief from his pocket and dabbing her eyes and cheeks.

"Don't touch her," Anna snapped.

"And you're the feisty one, I see," Samuel said, stepping up to Anna. "I think we'll have to tame you."

Angered, Anna kicked Samuel in the shin and yelled, "Run, Emma, run." She pushed past Samuel and Albert and ran towards the gaggle at the end of the dock; but just before she reached them, she leapt from the dock and landed on the edge of the shoreline.

Emma was frozen in fear and remained where she stood.

"Get her!" Albert barked.

Immediately, a half-dozen men went in pursuit of Anna.

Agile and quick, Anna steadied herself and sprinted towards a tree line forty feet away. She glanced over her shoulder and saw Emma wasn't coming. Should she stay? Or should she keep running? Never had she faced such a dilemma. She then caught sight of the men coming and fast. It took her seconds to reach the tree line. Once there, she darted back and forth around old-growth hardwoods. Behind her, she could hear the men coming, but she had made up her mind. She'd escape, find help, and come back for Emma. Once again, she glanced over her shoulder and saw she was pulling away from the pack of men. When she put her attention back to where she was going, the tip of her shoe clipped a fallen log. She toppled to the ground hard, impaling her shoulder on a branch. "Argh!" she cried out in pain.

"She's over here!" one of the men hollered and pointed in Anna's direction.

Anna got back to her feet, the branch still imbedded in her shoulder. She looked and saw the men closing; her spill had closed the gap considerably. The pain from the branch in her shoulder was shooting through her upper body, but she wouldn't let it stop her. She took off again.

Using every ounce of energy she had, she once more began to pull away from the men. She exited the woods onto a dirt road. Looking both ways, she spotted a covered wagon coming from the right. This was what she needed. She sprinted towards it. "Help!" she yelled, waving her good arm.

A lone man was driving the wagon. He pulled back on the reins to stop the wagon. "Whoa."

"Help, please help me!" Anna hollered, running up to the man.

"What's wrong, girl…oh, wait, you're injured," the man said. He was older, in his sixties. He held his hand out to help Anna step onto the wagon. "What happened?"

"We need to go now. Those men are coming to get me," she screamed and pointed farther down the road as the men began to spill out of the wood and onto the road.

"Those men?" the old man asked.

"Yes, now go, hurry!" she cried out.

The old man shook his head and laughed.

"Go!" Anna yelled.

"I can't go on account I work for those men," the

old man said, pulling out a pistol and putting it to Anna's head. "Sorry, little lady, I think you're my cargo today."

Anna's heart sank upon hearing those words leave the old man's mouth.

"You be a good girl and just sit there. Don't give me a reason to shoot ya," the old man said.

"Please let me go, please," Anna pleaded.

The men who had exited the woods saw the old man and the wagon and began to wave at him.

"I got her here!" the old man hollered back.

"Please, my pa is rich, very rich. If you let me go, he will pay you," Anna begged.

"How rich?" the old man asked.

"Very rich, he owns a railroad."

The old man's brows rose. Anyone who owned a railroad wasn't just rich, they were filthy rich. "How do you reckon I get you out of here now?"

"You said I was your cargo. Take us somewhere safe."

"Us?" the old man asked, his eyes darting back and forth between Anna and the men racing towards him.

"My sister is also a prisoner. I will have my pa give you a lot of money if you can take us somewhere safe and make sure we get home," Anna begged.

"How much?"

"As much as you can imagine," she said frantically, hoping to make a deal before the others showed up.

"I have a good imagination. How about ten thousand?" he asked.

"Yes, he can easily pay you that," Anna said.

"Damn, I went too low. How about fifteen?" the old man asked.

"Yes, just tell me you'll help me and my sister," Anna said, the men closing in fast.

"I'll help you," the old man said and gave her a wink.

The men arrived out of breath, with one walking over towards the right side of the wagon and taking a hold of Anna's arm. He cocked a clenched fist back but was stopped by another man.

"We can't hurt her," one of the men said.

"She's already hurt bad," another man blurted out as he pointed at Anna's shoulder.

The old man hollered, "Jump in the back. I need to get her to the dock and get her cleaned up. Poor thing has a branch stuck in her shoulder."

One by one, the men climbed into the back.

The old man gave Anna a look and whispered, "I'll get you patched up; then we'll get you home safe."

"Thank you," Anna said.

"What's your name?" the old man asked.

"Anna."

"My name is Clay. Nice to meet ya."

CHICAGO, ILLINOIS

Milton Wallace had been with the Pinkerton Detective Agency for over fifteen years, so when he heard the director of operations, a man by the name of Baxter Gillian, wished to speak to him personally, he knew the importance of the meeting.

Milton stopped at the door just before knocking and smoothed his hair, ensuring not a strand was out of place, for Gillian was known to scrutinize every employee he came across, including their hair.

He cleared his throat and practiced what he'd say upon meeting Gillian. Ready to go, he knocked.

"Enter!" Gillian hollered.

Milton opened the heavy door and stepped inside the massive office that controlled a commanding view of Lake Michigan.

"Ah, Milton Wallace, just the man I needed to see. Come in and take a seat," Gillian said, motioning to a lone chair in front of the desk.

Milton saw another man was sitting next to it, but didn't recognize him.

"Don't be shy. Come on in," Gillian said, closing a folder and laying it on a stack of others.

Milton walked in and took a seat. He glanced at the burly man seated next to him and nodded.

The man didn't respond. He gave Milton a hard stare then put his attention back on Gillian.

"Mr. Wallace, this is Ulysses Harrison; he's a new hire. Used to work for the United States Marshals Service."

"Hello, Mr. Harrison," Milton said, hoping a more formal greeting would be returned.

Harrison said, "How do you do?"

"I'm swell, thank you, and welcome to the Pinkerton Detective Agency," Milton said.

"Mr. Harrison, you know why you're here, but let me

bring you up to speed, Mr. Wallace," Gillian said, taking a folder and opening it up. "We received a telegram from a Mr. Fulton, who has requested our services immediately to help find his two daughters he believes were abducted. We're sending you both down to Topeka to meet with him tomorrow. You should arrive by the late afternoon or evening, I can't remember, but your tickets are in here," Gillian said, sliding the folder to Milton. "You've been with us for a long time; you know how to handle these sorts of cases."

"Yes, sir, I do," Milton said.

"And, Harrison, I expect you'll follow Wallace's lead on this case. He's the senior agent. Do you understand?"

"Yes, sir," Harrison said, his voice rough and deep.

"Good. I also expect you to handle this case with the utmost discretion. Mr. Fulton is a well-known man, and we must ensure that his privacy is maintained throughout. If you have any issues or questions, telegram us immediately."

"Of course, sir," Milton said.

"There are two girls out there missing; track them down and find them. Your mission is not to bring those responsible to justice," Gillian said.

"We will do our jobs, sir, as we always do, but I'm not clear on what you just meant," Milton said.

"This case has the attention of the president of our company. It was he who put Mr. Harrison on it, and he's told me your sole job is to find the girls—don't get sidetracked with tracking down any perpetrators. Of course, if you need to use deadly force, do so in the line of protecting yourselves, the general public and the girls."

"But if we have one of the kidnappers, we're not to capture them and turn them over to the local authorities?" Milton asked.

"That's not your job; it's solely to find the girls and bring them back safely," Gillian said. "Listen, Mr. Wallace, I know this flies in the face of the other cases and how we've handled them."

"But—" Milton protested but was stopped before he could finish.

"Mr. Wallace, do you understand the parameters of the job?"

"Yes," Milton answered.

"Are you or aren't you willing to follow them? If you're not, I can assign someone else. Let me know now, as there are two girls out there that need our help," Gillian blared.

"I'll follow them," Milton said. He wanted to protest more, but after Gillian's impassioned retort, he quieted himself.

"Good, and I know you will, Mr. Wallace; you're a good man and agent. And I like the suit; you look good," Gillian said.

"Thank you, sir," Milton said.

"You both can go," Gillian said.

Wallace and Milton stood up simultaneously.

"Sir, I have another question. Can I have a word with you in private?" Milton asked.

"Only if you promise it's not concerning what we just discussed," Gillian said.

"It's not," Milton promised.

Harrison nodded and left the office.

When the door closed, Milton said, "Sir, this case, the client is an important man."

"All of our clients are important," Gillian said, shuffling papers on his desk.

"I understand that, sir, but why are you sending me with a new agent?" Milton asked.

Looking up, Gillian replied, "He may be new to the agency, but he's an experienced United States Marshal and familiar with tracking down some of the most wanted in the country. He's a seasoned law enforcement official, and we're lucky to have him in our ranks now."

"I understand that, but—"

"And his appointment to this case came from up top; he's on the case. Why don't you stop worrying about such things and go pack your things?" Gillian said.

"You didn't pick him for this?" Milton asked.

Gillian grunted and said, "No, I didn't, but it doesn't matter. I spoke to him just before you arrived, and I had an opportunity to look at his record. He's an asset to this case. Now if you're done questioning how the staffing is done, I need to get back to work."

"I'm finished, sir, thank you," Milton said and headed for the door.

"And, Wallace, do find those girls as fast as you can. I heard Mr. Fulton is also hiring some grungy bounty hunters, the lowest of the low. Please don't let them track those girls down before you do," Gillian sneered.

"I won't let you down, sir," Milton said then left.

SOUTH OF LEBANON, MISSOURI

Gavin's feet ached and his stomach clenched from hunger. He thought himself a fit young man and hadn't thought twice when he ran off the night before, but after walking the countless miles, he began to wonder if he was capable of making it all the way to Jefferson City.

The sun's light was about to retreat below the horizon, leaving him in the darkness of the night, but thankfully his father had shown him how to navigate via the stars and constellations.

In his rush to run away, he'd forgotten to take the sack of money he'd saved for years, a mistake that he was regretting with every fiber of his body.

The light and crackle of a fire off in the brush got his attention. He stopped to get a better look. Through the thick tall grasses and heavy branches, he could see two men, but more importantly he saw a rabbit cooking above the flames. His mouth watered when he imagined chewing the moist meat. He thought about approaching them and asking if they'd spare some food, then thought about the stories his father had told him while they'd work the fields. He'd recounted tales of road agents and bandits living along the sides of the roads and trails. Were these men bandits? he asked himself. He didn't know, and the fear caused by those tales prevented him from even trying. He remembered seeing a handwritten sign that read Lebanon Four Miles. Maybe he could walk into town and find a generous hand to help him out and spare some food. Thinking this was his best bet, he stood up from his hiding place, turned and stepped. His trousers snagged a branch and caused him to crash to the ground.

The men around the fire heard the snapping branches of his fall and called out, "Who goes there?"

Gavin didn't move. He lay on the ground where he fell, hoping they'd think nothing of all the noise he'd made.

The men talked amongst each other and decided one would go out to look.

Hearing this, fear gripped Gavin. *What should I do?* he thought. *Should I get up and run or take my chances and hope they don't see me in the dark?* He opted to remain still.

The lone man took a torch and made towards the source of the sound.

Gavin clasped his hands together and began to pray.

"Who's out here? Come on out," the man barked, his voice rough and deep.

Should I run, should I? Gavin asked himself.

The man closed in. Each step he took brought him closer and closer to Gavin, the orange glow of the torch providing enough light to see. "Just come on out. We won't hurt you."

He's going to find me, I know it, Gavin thought, his eyes pressed closed.

The man was now just feet from Gavin. He waved the torch around and said, "I heard you. Now come on out."

"Well, did you find who made that sound?" the other man asked from the fire.

"No, nothing here. Must have been a deer or other

varmint," the man said.

"Come on back, then. The hare is ready," the man at the fire said.

"I'm coming," the man said, turning; then he saw something out of the corner of his eye. "Well, what do we have here?" He took a step closer to Gavin and leaned down.

Gavin opened his eyes and saw the man reaching for him. Terror shot through him. He sprang to his feet, turned and ran right into a thick bush.

The man began to laugh loudly. "Boy, what in the hell are you doing?"

"Whatcha got there, Finnegan?" the man called out from the fire.

"A boy, by the looks of it, a scared one at that," Finnegan replied, laughing.

"Well, what does he want?"

"Don't know. He's a bit preoccupied in a bush right now," Finnegan answered.

Gavin struggled to free himself from the entanglement of the bush but was having a hard time. He cried out, "Don't hurt me. Please don't hurt me."

"Boy, we're not in the business of hurting anyone," Finnegan said.

It was then that Gavin noticed that Finnegan and the other man had accents he'd never heard before.

"Boy, calm down and let me help you out of that bush," Finnegan said.

"Are you a bandit? Do you mean me harm?" Gavin cried out in fear.

"No, boy, we're priests. We're on our way to Jefferson City from Little Rock, Arkansas," Finnegan replied.

"Priests?" Gavin asked.

"I swear to the heavenly Father that is who we are," Finnegan said.

Gavin slowed his thrashing and craned his head back to see the man was wearing a black shirt with a white frock. "You are a priest."

Finnegan nodded and asked, "Now how about I help you out of that nasty bush?"

***

Gavin tore off a big chunk of thigh meat with his teeth and chewed. A broad smile stretched across his face each time he ground his teeth into the meat.

"When was the last time you ate, son?" Finnegan asked, giving a wink to his colleague, Aidan.

With his mouth full, Gavin replied, "Last night."

"Are you without a home?" Aidan asked.

"No, Father, I'm heading to Jefferson City myself. I have an apprenticeship there waiting for me," Gavin replied.

"Jefferson City, aye, I hear it's a nice city," Aidan said. "The diocese there needs priests, so we've been sent from our old parish in Little Rock."

"We gave you a fright, didn't we?" Finnegan asked.

"Yes, you did," Gavin replied, taking another big bite.

"Care for some ale?" Aidan asked, holding up a jug.

"Sure," Gavin said.

Aidan passed the jug to Gavin, who took it and carefully poured some into his mouth. As he swallowed, he coughed slightly. He handed the jug back to Aidan and said, "Thank you."

"Ever had ale before?" Aidan asked.

"No, Father, that would be the first time," Gavin said.

"Take another drink, then," Aidan said.

Gavin took the jug again and drank, this time not coughing. "It's good."

"We make it ourselves, at least we did back at our parish in Little Rock."

"Are you walking to Jefferson City?" Finnegan asked. "I didn't see a horse."

"Yes."

Finnegan gave Aidan a look then put his attention back on Gavin and said, "How about you accompany us to Jefferson City? We have been blessed with a wagon and we have the room. You can ride in the back."

Gavin's eyes widened with joy. "You don't mind?"

"It's the godly thing to do. I say you camp with us; then join us in the morning. We hope to arrive in Jefferson City by midday tomorrow," Finnegan said.

"If I'm not imposing, yes, I'd love to ride with you," Gavin said. He could hardly believe his luck. He'd initially thought these men were road agents or bandits, and they turned out to be the opposite: God-fearing priests.

"That is wonderful. You see, Aiden, I told you we'd

find a weary soul along this trail, and here he is. God puts us in front of those in need, and we help. It's destiny," Finnegan said.

"Agreed, Finn," Aidan said. "But what is our weary traveler's name?"

"Gavin, my name is Gavin."

"Gavin, I'm Father Howard, and this lad here is Father Leary," Aidan said.

"You sound different," Gavin said.

"Ha, I think you sound different." Finnegan laughed.

"We're from Ireland, emigrated five years ago from Dublin. We first stepped foot on American soil in Galveston, Texas, then headed to Little Rock," Aidan said.

"I've never met anyone from Ireland before," Gavin said.

"Fortunately for us, there's more than a few of us here. Unfortunately there's also many Englishmen here too," Finnegan joked.

Aidan and Finnegan laughed. Gavin sat, not knowing what the joke meant.

The three finished eating and prepared for sleep.

"Are you a Catholic?" Aidan asked.

"No, Father, I'm Baptist," Gavin replied.

"No matter, I'm glad we could be of help to you," Aidan said. "Good night, Gavin."

"Good night, lad," Finnegan said.

"Good night," Gavin said. He closed his eyes and once more counted his blessings. Within seconds he was fast asleep.

OLATHE, KANSAS

Fisk arrived at the dining hall late. He frantically looked around, hoping Abigail and Dwight would still be there.

Seeing Fisk scanning the room, Dwight raised his arm and called out, "Here."

Fisk rushed over and began to apologize. "Please forgive my tardiness. I got back to my hotel room and found I had a telegram urging me to go to Topeka right away to cover the big abduction case. I told them I needed tonight; then I'll head there in the morning." He pushed his utensils out of the way and placed down a notebook. He opened it, took out a pencil, and wrote a few words on the page. "Can I start with you, Abigail?"

Abigail watched him curiously. She hadn't been properly interviewed before and wasn't sure if she would enjoy talking about herself. She never much liked it, but knowing this would be shared made her feel even more reluctant. If it weren't for Dwight wanting the publicity, she would have said no.

"Abigail?" Fisk said, noticing she wasn't paying attention.

"Yes," Abigail replied.

"Can I start with you?" Fisk asked again.

As if on cue, a waiter appeared. "Can I get you something to drink?"

Dwight said, "I'll take another whiskey."

"Root beer for me," Abigail said.

"I'll just have a beer, please," Fisk said.

The waiter nodded and promptly left.

"Root beer? I heard you don't drink alcohol. Why is that?" Fisk asked.

"On account my father was a drunk," she answered bluntly.

Fisk laughed then jotted something into his notebook.

"What's so funny?" Abigail asked.

"How people answer that question. It's usually one or the other. I'd like to know for sure how it breaks, if it's fifty-fifty or sixty-forty."

"What do you mean?" Abigail asked, her state shifting from curiosity to annoyance.

"I can tell by your tone that you think I'm poking fun; I'm not. What I mean is that when someone has a parent who was an alcoholic, the children will either follow in their footsteps or not drink at all."

"What about those who drink but have the self-control not to become drunks?" Abigail asked.

Fisk furrowed his brow and said, "I never thought of that."

"Maybe you should, instead of making foolish comments," Abigail snapped.

"Abby, he didn't mean anything by it," Dwight said.

"I didn't really, I swear," Fisk said.

The waiter returned with their drinks and placed them in front of each one. "Have you had a chance to look at the menu?"

"Please come back in a few minutes," Dwight said.

The waiter nodded and walked away.

"How about we start again. Um, tell me about who

you are and where you came from," Fisk asked.

Abigail shook her head and said, "Dwight, I really don't want to do this. You know how important it is to keep our anonymity."

"He won't use our real names, will you?" Dwight asked Fisk.

"Of course not. I can't on account I don't know them," Fisk replied.

"Still, I don't really want to do this," Abigail said.

"Why?" Dwight asked.

"I'm a bounty hunter; that's who I am. I'm not here for fame," she answered.

"Why not?" Dwight asked.

Fisk sat back and watched the back-and-forth.

"On account this is wasting time. We should be looking for our next job, not sitting here…doing this. No offense to you," she said to Fisk.

"None taken," Fisk said with a smile.

"Abigail, you promised we would try to get publicity if we could," Dwight said, his tone showing he was becoming aggravated with her.

Abigail sighed, looked at Fisk, and rattled off a few quick facts about herself. "I was born in Montana, a small town I won't name on account of my previous comments. My mother died after giving birth to me, and my father abused me all my life. When I wasn't being abused by him, I spent a considerable amount of time with my aunt and uncle. My uncle Billy taught me how to shoot, ride, use a knife, throw a tomahawk, and let me wear pants all the time. After his murder, I sought out his old partner Hammer Tillis so I could recruit him to go after the man who killed them. That was my first job. Since then I've completed twenty other jobs, with the capture of Ted McKnight being my latest."

"Twenty-two," Dwight said, correcting her.

"Fine, twenty-two," Abigail said.

Fisk was busy writing everything down. When he was done, he looked at his notes and asked, "Where is your father?"

"Dead," she answered.

"How did he die?" Fisk asked.

"Is that important?" she answered, not wanting to ever divulge she had killed him.

"I suppose not. What can you tell me about Hammer Tillis? He had quite the reputation as a killer; often skirting the line between law and order."

"I knew him as Grant Toomey; he'd changed his name after meeting his wife. They moved to Idaho and he became a potato farmer. The man you're talking about never crossed my path. I knew him as kind, wise…he was a good man."

"He died on that job you did in Montana, correct?"

"As far as I know, yes. And as it refers to Grant, I expect you to keep his real name out of your article, I don't need his family bothered because you ran his name in the newspaper."

Fisk scratched out the passage referring to Grant and said, "Of course. Now, when did you and Dwight become partners?" Fisk asked.

"Do you mind if I answer that?" Dwight asked

Abigail.

"Go ahead," she said, reaching for her root beer.

"I'd heard about her a couple of months before we ran into each other outside Dallas. She was in a bit of trouble and I came to help. After that we talked about partnering, with her quickly dashing the idea until a year ago. Since then we've been working quite well together."

"A bit of trouble? I had that situation under control," Abigail said, her brow raised and her head cocked.

"There were three men and you had run out of ammunition. I call that a bit of trouble," Dwight said, reminding her of the specifics of that job.

"I had my pistol and I had a plan," Abigail said.

"And that was?" Dwight asked, sitting back. He looked forward to her response.

Abigail paused. She gave Fisk a quick look and saw he was enjoying the banter. Not wanting to give him anything that could hurt them or give the wrong impression, she relented. "I would have figured it out, as I always have, but having you to back me up certainly helped, and for that I'm grateful."

"So you needed his help?" Fisk asked, hoping to prod the disagreement forward.

"I'll say this, no matter what, I would have prevailed against Tom and his gang, but having Dwight show up and help no doubt put an end to the job quicker."

"Was that a yes or a no?" Fisk asked.

Seeing that Abigail was attempting to walk the line, Dwight backed her up. "Abby is one of the most proficient shots and smartest bounty hunters riding today.

I have no doubt she would have taken Tom and his men out; I merely sped up the process."

"But you said she was in trouble," Fisk said, reminding Dwight of his earlier comment.

"What I meant was that I perceived then she was in a bit of trouble, so I jumped in and helped her return fire."

"I see," Fisk said, jotting down more notes.

Abigail leaned forward, reached across the table, and took Fisk's writing hand. "I suggest you write this story ensuring you keep us both in a proper light." She gave him a hard look and continued, "I'd hate to read later that you slandered me or Dwight."

Fisk gulped and said, "I'd never dream of slandering either of you."

"Good," Abigail said with a smile and leaned back in her chair.

Fisk continued to ask questions, mainly focusing on the jobs they'd done and life on the trail, with Abigail and Dwight both answering as truthfully as they could.

They eventually ordered dinner and had it brought to the table. Even with a large plate of food in front of him, Fisk continued to pepper them with questions.

When he was done, he pushed his plate aside and said, "I think we've covered all of your jobs." Looking through his notebook, he gushed, "I've gotten a lot of good information here. My readers are going to love it."

"Good," Abigail said.

"I'll be excited to read it when it goes to print," Dwight said. "When do you suppose that will be?"

"You should expect the first article to hit in a couple

of weeks," Fisk answered.

"Then I suppose we're done," Abigail said, pushing her chair away from the table.

"Wait. I do have another question," Fisk said.

Abigail stopped and waited.

"You…and your partner tend to kill your targets versus take them alive. I've heard your explanation as to why, and on its face, it does make sense. The question I have is how do you deal with so much killing?"

Abigail and Dwight both shared a look. She cleared her throat and said, "We value our lives more than those criminals or outlaws. As you know, we've taken some targets alive…"

"I know that, and that was because it was mandated, but when you're given the option, you kill them," Fisk said.

"Like we've explained, it's easier to kill a man then take his body to the authorities. Granted, on some we get paid half, but the risk is averted. If you're asking how we deal with so much killing, I'll simply say the world is a better place without these people. Most of the times those whom we bring back alive get tried then subsequently hanged. Death is a part of life, period, and dying young or being killed is very much a part of the life of an outlaw. They know this and so do we. We accept that fact. Anyone who lives by the gun tends to die by the gun."

Fisk smiled broadly. "Great answer. Let me ask, then, do you believe you'll die by the gun?"

"I don't plan on dying at all," Dwight joked.

"What about you?" Fisk asked Abigail.

"I'm aware that what I do is dangerous and any day I could get killed. I don't worry about it. If I were to die tomorrow, I know I've had a positive impact because of what I do."

"You're not afraid of dying?" Fisk asked.

"No, I'm not. Mind you, I don't want to die, so don't be mistaken. This isn't to say I don't get nervous or scared going into a fight; I do. But the thought of death itself doesn't faze me. If it did, I wouldn't do this job."

"Another great answer," Fisk said, excited.

"Did you get what you need?" Abigail asked.

"Where will you both go now?" Fisk asked.

Again, Dwight and Abigail shared a look.

"We don't know yet, but I'll do some research to find another bounty we should pursue," Dwight answered.

"May we continue this process going forward, say in six months?" Fisk asked.

"Sure," Dwight said.

Abigail remained silent, her attention on the others in the dining hall.

Fisk stuck out his hand. "It's been a pleasure and thank you."

Dwight and Abigail both shook his hand.

Fisk jumped to his feet, picked up and cradled his things, then rushed off as frantically as he'd arrived.

"I'm glad that's over," Abigail said.

"You did great. In fact, you answered more questions and were very open about your life, more so than I thought you would be."

"I'm glad you're happy," Abigail quipped.

"You're a good partner. Thanks for doing that," Dwight said.

"I'm tired. I want to go to sleep," Abigail said, rising to her feet and stretching.

"Like he asked, where to next?" Dwight asked.

"Right now I don't care. All I want to see is the back of my eyelids." Abigail yawned.

"Then let's see what fate brings us," Dwight said.

KANSAS CITY, MISSOURI

Anna could hear the distinct sound of water moving from beneath the sack that covered her head. She didn't have any idea where or how long she'd been in the wagon after having passed out minutes after being loaded onto it, but if she were to guess, she'd say they were still near the river. Her shoulder was bandaged but sore, and a heavy fatigue weighed on her small body. She wasn't sure if the deal she'd struck with Clay was going to be honored, unless she'd missed something during her slumber.

Voices came from outside the wagon. It was Clay and another voice that she recalled hearing from earlier today. It was tough to make out, but it sounded as if Clay was negotiating with the other man. Seconds later the mundane conversation turned to shouting then a gunshot.

"What's happening?" Emma cried out.

Anna reached out with her good arm until she found Emma. "It's okay. Soon we'll be rescued."

"I don't know. I think we're going to die; this is it," Emma whined.

"Stop saying things like that," Anna said. She was tired of Emma's negative attitude. Yes, they were in a precarious position but only so because of Emma. If they were going to escape, Emma had to equip herself with hope and a positive demeanor.

The flap on the covered wagon opened. Clay stuck his head inside and said, "Almost there."

"What happened?" Anna asked.

"He didn't agree with the deal," Clay said then closed the flap.

The wagon continued forward for what seemed like an eternity before it stopped again.

Anna listened intently and could hear what sounded like steam coming from a train's engine.

"I hear a train," Emma said.

"Me too," Anna replied.

"Where are they taking us?" Emma asked.

"Emma, I made a deal with the old man. He's going to rescue us. Just be patient," Anna said.

"We're going home?" Emma asked.

"Yes."

Clay jumped from the wagon and walked off. He returned shortly with three other men.

Anna heard them approach and was happy to know that soon her and Emma's ordeal would be over.

The flap opened, and in came the bright orange glow of an oil lantern. "There's two, boss."

Anna didn't recognize that voice. Who was this?

Were they going to help?

"Francois, pull them girls out," a voice called out.

"Stand up and walked towards me," Francois said with a heavy creole accent.

Anna and Emma did as he said and were soon standing on what felt like loose gravel.

Unexpectedly, the sacks were ripped from their heads. The bright light of a lantern briefly blinded them. A tall and lanky man walked up, took the lantern from Francois, and held it close to the girls' faces. "Oh, they're perfect. I'm happy Clay decided to bring them to us."

Anna was confused. She looked around until she saw Clay counting coins from a sack. "What's happening? Clay, what's going on?"

Clay looked up and smiled. He held the sack high and said, "This was a certain payment. No hard feelings."

Anna lowered her head, distraught. She had sworn Clay would help, but apparently the bird in the hand was a better deal. "You lied."

Clay walked up and lifted her face. "Sorry, but let me give you a bit of advice. If you want to survive, be smart."

Another man pushed his way past Francois and the tall man and stopped inches from the girls; he gave Clay a stern look and snapped, "You've been paid. Move on."

Clay tipped his hat and said just before walking away, "Always a pleasure doing business with you, Jacques."

"Baron is going to fall in love with these two. Get them on the train now," Jacques ordered, snapping his fingers.

Francois stepped forward, took both girls by the

arms, and escorted them to a train car. One by one, he picked them up and put them on board. "Make yourself comfortable." He laughed, slamming the heavy door closed and locking it.

Encased in the darkness, Anna and Emma both looked around but saw nothing.

"I'm scared," Emma said, clinging to Anna.

"Me too," Anna said.

"Psst, you two, over here," a voice from the darkness called out.

"Who's that?" Anna asked, looking but unable to see anything.

"My name is Evelyn. I'm a prisoner like you. Walk over to your left; we're in the corner," Evelyn said.

Unsure of what to do, Anna replied, "You're a prisoner?"

"Yes, I was taken two days ago in Omaha," Evelyn said.

Anna grabbed Emma's hand and walked slowly towards her voice. They ran into the far wall of the car first, then made their way towards Evelyn's voice until they came upon the group of children huddled together. Their small bodies were trembling from fear.

"Do you know who these men are?" Anna asked.

"Don't know. I've heard a few names mentioned, but what's going to become of us is unknown," Evelyn said.

"I want my mommy," a girl said, her voice cracking with terror.

"It'll be okay, Mary," Evelyn said softly, hoping her words would console her.

The train car jerked forward, startling everyone, then began to slowly move.

"Where are we going?" Anna asked.

"To die," a girl by the name of Ashley said.

"I think they're going to sell us as slaves," a girl named Sarah blurted out.

Anna and Emma sat on the dirty floor. Emma placed her head between her legs and began to sob. Rubbing her back, Anna said, "Don't cry, sister."

"How old are you?" Evelyn asked.

"Fourteen. Both of us are," Anna said.

"Twins?" Evelyn asked.

"Yes, I'm the oldest by a few minutes," Anna said.

"I'm thirteen," Evelyn said. "Sarah is twelve, Ashley is too, and Mary is thirteen."

"Just the four of you?" Anna asked.

"Now six with you two," Evelyn said.

"I want to go home," Mary cried out.

"Soon you will," Anna declared.

Evelyn leaned in and whispered, "Don't say things like that."

"Why?" Anna asked.

"Just don't," Evelyn replied.

Ignoring Evelyn's cautious approach, Anna said, "I was close to escaping once. I'll try again, I promise you, I will."

CHAPTER THREE

OLATHE, KANSAS

APRIL 9, 1891

Before Abigail took the last step into the lobby of the hotel, she saw Fisk sitting anxiously near the front door, his head down, writing. She grunted and wondered what he wanted. Hoping to slip by without him noticing, she turned her head away from him and darted towards the dining hall, praying she could eat breakfast in peace.

Her prayers went unanswered, as Fisk looked up and spotted her crossing the wide lobby. "Miss Abigail," he called out, waving his hand feverishly.

Abigail ignored him and kept walking.

Fisk jumped to his feet, pushed his way past a few guests standing in the lobby, and hurried after her. "Abigail."

Knowing she'd never get to a table without addressing what he wanted, she sighed loudly and turned around. "Yes, what can I do for you?"

"You seem angry," Fisk said, taken aback by her response.

"Not angry, more like annoyed," she said.

Several people sitting in the dining hall gave Abigail a glance, not because of her tone but due to her attire. As usual, she was wearing trousers, a buttoned-up shirt, and a vest. Around her waist, her gun belt hung snugly.

She caught sight of a man scowling and sneered, "You have something to say to me?"

The man quickly turned away and went back to his breakfast.

"I need to tell you something, something I know you'll have great interest in," Fisk said.

"I'll tell you what, you can tell me, but you have to agree to pick up breakfast," she said.

"But I've already eaten," he said.

"Then I'm not interested," she said and walked off. She found a table near the back and sat down.

Fisk chased after her. He chuckled when he arrived at the table and said, "Of course I'll pay for your meal."

"Then sit," she said, motioning towards the chair opposite her.

"Ah, where is Dwight?"

"Not sure," she said, waving towards a waiter.

"Too bad he's not here. I so wanted to tell both of you at the same time," Fisk said, knowing that Dwight would respond more positively to his news.

"Well, he's not, sorry," she said.

"You seem to be in a bad mood," Fisk said.

"I'm not. It's just that I don't trust, much less like, reporters. I've often found they lie or misrepresent the information they're entrusted to report," she replied.

Fisk smiled and said, "It's unfortunate, but we're human and, yes, I'd agree many who claim journalism as a profession fail to leave their personal biases at home, often taking them to their place of business and even going as far as spreading falsehoods."

"We agree on something," Abigail said.

The waiter arrived and asked, "What can I get for you?" He gave Abigail a judgmental look before turning his attention to Fisk.

"Oh, I'm not eating, but I'll take a cup of coffee," Fisk answered the waiter.

"And what will *you* have?" the waiter sneered at Abigail.

"What is it this morning with this place? Last night went by without an odd look; this morning everyone's giving me the evil eye."

"On account of your attire…madam," the waiter said.

"What's wrong with how I'm dressed?" Abigail asked, sitting back in her chair and crossing one leg over the other like a man.

"By societal standards, you're dressed inappropriately, that's all I'll say," the waiter replied, standing tall and rigid.

"How do you think I should dress?" Abigail asked.

"Like a lady…ma'am," the waiter answered.

Abigail leaned forward, placed her elbows on the table, and motioned the waiter with her hands to come closer.

He leaned down and waited.

"Thing is, I'm not a lady, I'm a bounty hunter, a hired gun, and if you give me any more guff or preach to me about societal morals, attire, etcetera, I'll take this Colt here and blow off your family jewels, effectively turning *you* into a…lady," Abigail said sternly, her right hand touching the back strap of her pistol. "Now run off and get me two eggs fried, bacon, toast, and a cup of coffee."

Flustered and frightened by her response, the waiter rushed off.

Fisk laughed loudly.

"What's so funny?" Abigail asked.

"That…that was hilarious. How you handled him, it was brilliant, truly breathtaking to watch you work. I'm truly blessed and honored to be in your presence," Fisk replied.

His response made her feel better about him. She leaned back and asked, "What do you need to tell me?"

"Oh yes, that. I have your next job," he said happily.

"Go on," she said.

"Remember yesterday I told you I'd received a telegram from my editor, telling me to rush to Topeka because of a missing persons case? Well, I received more information on it. Two girls have gone missing, presumed abducted—"

"That sounds like a case for the law to handle," Abigail said, interrupting him.

"The police and county sheriff are involved, as are Pinkerton detectives; however, the father and mother are desperate. I telegrammed my editor late last night informing them of an idea I had. I also took the liberty to telegram the parents of the family and told them about…" Fisk said then paused.

"About?"

"You."

"Me?"

"You can find anyone, and I think you can find these missing girls," Fisk said. "Anyway, I received a reply from the parents this morning. They want to hire you, but first want to meet you."

Stunned, Abigail looked off and thought. She enjoyed her job immensely, but what she cared about more was helping children, specifically ones that could be in the hands of abusive adults. If she could bring her expertise to bear, she should take the job, no matter what.

"If you take this job, and I hear it pays very well, I get to come with you and document the entire thing," Fisk said. "Consider that my finder's fee."

She glanced at him and said, "You have a deal." She jumped to her feet and headed out of the dining hall.

Shocked, Fisk got up and raced after her. "You'll do it?" he cried out loudly.

Heads in the dining hall turned and stared at Fisk.

She stopped in the lobby and answered Fisk. "Yes, I'll do it."

"Do what?" Dwight said from midway up the stairwell.

Abigail turned to him and answered, "Go pack. I have our next job."

"You do?" Dwight asked, a look of surprise on his face.

"Yes, and there's no time to waste," Abigail said, pushing past him on the stairs on her way to her room.

"Do I have time for breakfast?" Dwight asked.

"No, now go pack your stuff. We leave on the next train for Topeka," Abigail ordered.

Dwight glanced at Fisk, who stood in the lobby, gleaming with excitement. "What's going on?"

"Only the best thing that's ever happened to me," Fisk replied.

"Tell me this pays well," Dwight asked.

"Oh, it will, trust me," Fisk said. "Everyone is a winner on this job."

"Then I guess I'd better go pack my stuff," Dwight said and ran back up the stairs.

TOPEKA, KANSAS

Edward's temper flared upon hearing the news. "How is that possible?"

Thomas Myers, the timid and newly appointed chief of police, gripped his hat and lowered his gaze to the brightly colored Persian rug on the floor of Edward's office.

"Tell me, how is it no one can identify the man?" Edward asked.

"Sir, please don't yell," Thomas said.

"I should be doing more than yelling," Edward blared.

The double pocket doors of Edward's office opened, and in came Clara. "What's happened?"

Edward stared at her and replied, "Nothing, that's what's happened. Not a damn thing."

Clara's face tensed from seeing and hearing how upset Edward was. She was praying that the meeting with Thomas would provide critical information that could lead to finding the girls.

"Give me something, anything," Edward said.

"We know it was one man. The problem we're having is he didn't talk to any of the other children. Some of the children mentioned that they'd seen the man there the day before sitting on a bench. They said he never approached any of them. One boy said that when your girls arrived, he saw the man go and start talking to them right away. It's as if he was waiting for them."

"You're saying the girls were targeted, that this wasn't a random abduction?" Edward asked.

"Based on the evidence, which is scant, and the eyewitness testimony, yes, it just might be. I know you've given my investigators all the information on those who might have a grudge or wish harm to come to you, but I need to ask again if you can think of any reason, no matter how slight, that someone would want to do this," Thomas said.

"I haven't thought of anyone new, but the thing is, I've met so many people these past twelve months while getting my railroad started that I can't remember all the names. Did you interview the man who threatened me two months ago?" Edward asked, referring to a local man who had lost his land to eminent domain to make way for an easement for the railway.

"We did and he has an alibi, a solid one; plus he doesn't fit the description given to us by the other children," Thomas said, reaching into his pocket and removing a folded piece of paper. He walked over and handed it to Edward. "This is the composite sketch we have of the man. This was created from interviewing seven different children. They all agreed this is what the man looked like."

Edward took the paper, unfolded it, and stared at the image of the perpetrator. "I want this man found. I want him taken alive and the heavy hand of justice dealt, do you understand?" Edward said, tossing the paper on his desk.

Clara didn't budge though she was tempted to go look at the image.

"We're doing our best, Mr. Fulton; I've dedicated most of the police force to this case," Thomas said.

"Not all?" Edward asked.

"Sir, I can't do that. We have a responsibility to the entire city," Thomas said.

"I'll remind you that I contributed handsomely to your department. I expect something in return for my investment," Edward said.

"And you're getting it, sir," Thomas said.

"Anything else?" Edward asked.

Fidgeting with his hat, Thomas answered, "That was it. If I get anything else, no matter the time, I'll come straight over."

"Very well, thank you," Edward said, walking over and extending his hand. "I apologize for my outburst."

Thomas took his hand and shook it. "I understand your frustration. I'd be the same if I lost my little ones too."

"Sofie, escort the chief out!" Edward hollered to his head maid.

"I can show myself out, thank you," Thomas said, turned and exited. On his way past Clara, he nodded and said, "Good day, ma'am."

With Thomas gone, Clara closed the doors and rushed towards Edward's desk. The urge to see the sketch was too much to control. She snapped it up and stared into the squinting eyes of the man who took her girls. "We'll find you, we will, and when we do, I hope you suffer!" she growled. She spit on the sketch and threw it back on the desk.

Edward only watched. He knew it was important for her to get out her frustration and anger.

"When do the Pinkertons arrive?" Clara asked.

"Later today," he answered.

"And that woman bounty hunter?" she asked.

"I received a telegram just before the chief arrived. She's agreed to help us; she's on the next train here from Olathe. I expect her around the same time as the Pinkertons," Thomas replied.

"Good, whatever we need to spend, spend it, you hear me?" Clara snapped.

"Of course, dear, I'm doing everything I can," Edward said.

She walked up to Edward, pecked him on the cheek with a kiss, and said, "I want everyone involved to suffer. I want them to experience pain. I want to look them in the eye and…I want to hurt them myself. Then when I'm done, I want them dead."

Her anger shocked him, as he'd never seen or heard her like this, but then again, this situation was unique. He wasn't displeased with her behavior; on the contrary, he quite liked that she was willing to do whatever was necessary to find their girls, and if so be it, he'd use whatever means was in his power to ensure that justice was delivered.

JEFFERSON CITY, MISSOURI

The train came to a hard stop.

The children, still huddled together, woke and began to look around.

Sunlight crept through cracks and crevices in the railcar, giving them enough light to see by.

"Where are we?" Mary asked, rubbing her eyes.

"Don't any of us know," Evelyn said.

The sounds of chatter and walking could be heard outside the door of the railcar.

Sensing she might have a chance, Anna jumped to her feet and ran to the door. She stopped just beside it and waited in anticipation for it to open. On the floor at her feet she noticed a wooden slat was cracked. She bent down and pried a thick piece out and held it in her small hands. This would be a weapon for her to fight with.

"What are you doing?" Evelyn called out, she too getting to her feet.

"Emma, come with me…now!" Anna called out.

Still traumatized, Emma sat frozen. She glanced at Anna and shook her head.

"Emma, this might be our last chance," Anna barked. She ran back and knelt down. "Emma, please come with me. This is probably our last chance."

Emma didn't reply. She cradled her legs and shook her head. "No. We won't make it."

Frustrated, Anna snapped, "Emma, please!"

"She's right, you won't make it. These people know what they're doing; they'll catch you," Evelyn warned.

"How about stop being a pansy and help me," Anna snarled.

"I'm not a pansy," Evelyn protested.

The clack of metal sounded from the outside. It was the door being unlocked.

"Anna, don't leave me," Emma cried.

"This is our only chance. I'll come back for you. In the meantime I need you to be strong, stronger than you've ever been. Can you do that?" Anna asked.

"Please don't try to run, please," Emma begged.

"I have to. I need to go get help," Anna said and ran back to the door.

A clang followed by metal screaming came from the door.

Anna readied herself.

"But you won't know where I am. How will you find me?" Emma cried out.

The question struck Anna like a ton of bricks. Emma was right. If she managed to escape and find help, where would she tell them they were? Wait, the man last night had said something about Baron. That was a good clue. She didn't know whom it meant, but it was something to go on.

By the commotion outside, it sounded as if there

were several men.

Anna was now in a quandary. Should she try to escape or wait until a better time? But waiting until they got to where they were going had its negatives. Once there they'd be locked down for sure. No, this was the time; she was still out in the public domain. She could make a run for it and find help, possibly close by.

Sunlight began to slowly make its way into the railcar as the door opened inch by inch.

Anna clenched the sharp-edged piece of wood and stood ready to pounce.

The door fully opened.

Standing in front of Anna were Jacques and Francois. She kicked Jacques in the face, and using the sharp piece of wood, jammed it into Francois' neck. Both men were in shock, with Francois stumbling back from the railcar, blood flowing from the wound in his neck. He pulled the wood out, but it only made the bleeding worse.

Seeing her one chance, Anna jumped from the railcar, hit the ground soundly, and took off running. She could hear the men grumbling as well as the children cheering. Her heart pounded not only because she was running as fast as her legs could take her but because she knew what she had done could very well be a death sentence if caught.

A loud crack, which sounded like a gun firing, echoed.

Anna felt a searing pain in her abdomen but kept running. She turned right and onto a platform. Ahead of her about one hundred feet she saw a sign suspended from the ceiling of the walkway that read *OFFICE.*

Yelling soon erupted behind her, but this time she wasn't going to look back and see if anyone was following her. If she made it to the office, she could find help. The pain in her lower side was growing, but she chose to ignore it. She had to reach the office.

The door of the office opened, and out stepped a man dressed all in black and wearing a conductor's hat.

"Sir, help!" she cried out.

The man looked, his eyes wide. He turned towards her and said, "Oh my."

Anna reached him, wrapped her arms around his torso, and began to sob. "Help, please help."

The man looked down at her and said, "My, my, what's wrong, little girl."

The pain in Anna's side became overwhelming. She could feel a weakness spreading across her body. Using what little strength she had, she lifted her head and said, "Will you help me? I need to find my father."

"Of course, my dear," the man said, feeling awkward that Anna was clinging to him. "What's his name?"

"Edward Fulton, my father is Edward Fulton," Anna said then passed out from the pain and blood loss.

"Oh dear," the man said, shocked when Anna fell to the ground. He spotted the bloodstain on her lower right side and what appeared to be a small hole; he then realized she'd been shot. He scooped her up in his arms and raced off to get her medical attention.

TOPEKA, KANSAS

Abigail wasn't sure what to expect when she arrived at the Fulton residence. Dwight, on the other hand, only saw dollar signs for him when he laid his eyes on the grand house.

Leaning in close to Abigail, he whispered, "Let me lead with our fee for this one."

She nodded, not really concerned about such things at the moment.

They had been relegated to wait in the foyer as a butler went to inform Edward and Clara of their arrival.

Abigail used the time to look around the beautifully decorated and luxurious house. Voices from down the hall caught her attention. It sounded as if a woman was crying. Curious, she stepped away from Dwight and Fisk, who were busy talking, to explore and see what was going on. As she drew closer, she could now identify the cries coming from a woman.

"We must go now, Edward, we must," Clara begged.

"We are, trust me, my darling," Edward said.

"But what about my Emma? Are you sure it said only Anna?" Clara asked.

"Clara, go pack us some bags, hurry. I need to meet these people. Now go, hurry," Edward said, exiting the parlor to find Abigail nearby.

So as not to appear nosey, Abigail stood in front of a portrait and acted as if she were admiring it.

Edward walked up to her and said, "You must be Abigail."

Trying to feign surprise, Abigail replied, “Yes.”

Edward stuck out his hand and said, “Pleasure to meet you.”

Abigail took his hand and said, “The pleasure is mine.”

“We’ve just received urgent word concerning one of the girls. Please follow me to my office,” Edward said, motioning down the hall.

“Let me go get my partner,” Abigail said.

“Of course, do so, and meet me at the end of the hall. My office is there,” Edward said.

Abigail went and got Dwight and Fisk. They hurried to Edward’s office.

“Close the door,” Edward said the second they entered.

Fisk did as he said.

Edward stepped up to Dwight, hand extended, and said, “Edward Fulton.”

“Hi, I’m Dwight.”

“You two are the bounty hunters, and that gentleman there is the news reporter, correct?” Edward asked.

“How do you do?” Fisk asked.

“Honestly, not sure, we just received a telegram from Jefferson City, Missouri. My daughter Anna is there in a hospital. She’s been shot,” Edward said.

“And your other daughter?” Abigail asked.

“Nothing, only Anna, and she’s been unconscious since being found. We’re headed straight there on the train,” Edward said.

"What would you like us to do?" Dwight asked.

"I want you to find my other daughter. I need you to come to Jefferson City with me," Edward said.

Abigail gave Dwight a quick glance and said, "We'll need to bring our horses."

"Bring whatever you need. Just make sure you're ready to leave for the depot in fifteen minutes."

"Sir, there's the topic of our fee," Dwight said.

Abigail knew the timing was wrong and wanted to kick Dwight.

"Yes, the fee. I forgot this is a business transaction. To expedite these negotiations, I'll pay you three times your normal fee," Edward said.

Dwight's eyes widened. Tempted to go higher, he opened his mouth but was cut off.

"Deal," Abigail said.

Dwight sighed and shook his head slightly.

"Good, now let's prepare to leave," Edward said and hurried out of the office.

Ensuring he was gone, Dwight said, "We could've gotten more."

"We got a better than fair price for our work," Abigail said.

"But you know we can never take the first price offered," Dwight countered.

"Three times is fair," Abigail snapped.

"He can afford more," Dwight fired back.

"The deal is struck, now come on," Abigail said, walking away.

Like usual, Fisk stood taking in the back-and-forth.

Abigail stopped and said, "Don't think about adding any of this into your writing."

Wide-eyed, Fisk replied, "Oh, heavens no, I wouldn't think of it." Although deep down he was considering it.

"You're walking away from me and money, Abby," Dwight said.

Abigail swung and said, "No, Dwight, I'm taking a fair deal, and I'm not walking away, I'm walking in the direction of finding the one little girl that's still missing." In the hallway, Abigail saw Edward talking to two men dressed in black suits. They didn't look like business associates, and when one turned slightly, she saw the pistol on his hip.

Dwight came into the hall and asked, "Who are they?"

"I don't know, but I think Mr. Fulton has them on the payroll to help find his daughters too," Abigail answered.

Edward pointed at Abigail and Dwight then turned and headed upstairs. The men walked over. One was very large, making the other seem small though he wasn't by any standards a small man. "I presume you're Abigail?"

"Yes," Abigail said.

"And I'm Dwight, her partner," Dwight said, standing tall with one hand on the back strap of his Colt.

"I'm Milton Wallace, and this is Ulysses Harrison. We're with the Pinkerton Detective Agency. Mr. Fulton has hired us to find his daughters. I hear you're the famous Abby Sure Shot."

"More like infamous," Dwight joked.

Ignoring Dwight, Abigail said, "Just call me Abigail, or Abby, if you don't mind."

"I heard there was a couple of bounty hunters here. I didn't think one would be you," Milton said, giving Abigail a look from head to toe.

Harrison stood like a statue, not uttering a word.

"You're a quiet one," Dwight said to Harrison, who returned his comment with a disinterested glance.

"Ulysses here is a former US Marshal," Milton said.

"Nice to meet you, Ulysses," Abigail said, tipping her hat.

"Have you learned anything? As you can see, we've only just arrived," Milton said.

"Anna is in Jefferson City, Missouri. She's in a hospital due to a gunshot. We're headed that way shortly with Mr. Fulton," Abigail answered.

"He said we'd all be leaving soon," Milton said. "But has he discussed any of the details with you?"

"Not really, I expect to be briefed on the train," Abigail said. "And you, do you know anything you'd like to share with us?"

"Nothing, but if we learn something, we will be more than willing to offer that information to you, as long as you agree to reciprocate," Milton said.

"I think we could do that," Dwight said, not fearing who found Emma, as they would get paid either way.

"Good, I look forward to working with you both," Milton said and strutted off, with Harrison following close behind.

"He's lying," Abigail said.

"I know, but nothing wrong with being cordial," Dwight said, knowing Pinkertons were never known to work well with anyone outside of the agency.

"Let's just hope they don't get in our way," Abigail said.

JEFFERSON CITY, MISSOURI

When Gavin saw the city coming into view, his heart filled with pure joy. He'd made it. To be fair, he'd made it with the help of two priests.

"Where would you like us to drop you off?" Aidan asked.

"The Clancy Printing House, please," Gavin answered.

"Do you happen to know the address?" Aidan asked.

"I don't. I lost some of my belongings along the way," Gavin replied.

Aidan gave Finnegan a look. Finnegan nodded and said, "Do you have any money?"

"I'm ashamed that I don't. If I did, I'd repay you both for your generosity," Gavin said.

"Son, I wasn't asking so you could repay us, no; I was curious because a young man like yourself starting out in life shouldn't go to a strange town without some coin," Finnegan said, turning around and handing Gavin a small pouch.

Gavin looked at the pouch and then at Finnegan. "No, Father, I can't take your money."

Finnegan laughed. "It's not my money. It was given

to us so that we could put it to good use, and I think you would do just that."

Gavin felt awkward. "Are you sure, Father?"

"We are both sure," Finnegan said.

Aidan nodded.

Reluctantly, Gavin took the pouch and promptly slipped it into his pocket without counting it, as he thought that would be in bad taste.

"Now, when we enter the town limits, we'll find someone who can tell us where this Clancy Printing House is," Aidan said.

With each passing house, Gavin could not help but feel truly blessed. His adventure had started on a bad note with him having to run away, and now he was here in the city he'd make his future in, with a pocket full of money.

***

Finding the printing house was quite easy. Aidan pulled the wagon up to the front and stopped. "Clancy Printing House."

Gavin jumped out of the back and stared at the large two-story building near the far edge of town, a block from the river. He turned and said, "I want to thank you both. Without you I wouldn't have gotten here so quickly."

"You're very welcome," Finnegan said.

"I want to repay you. Please let me when I have come into the money," Gavin said.

"That is not necessary, we told you already. We're

not lending it to you, we're gifting it, which means it holds a different meaning. We no longer have possession of it; it's yours," Aidan said.

"I insist," Gavin said.

"I tell you what, why don't you pay us back by coming to mass on Sundays? You'll need some fellowship and some friends. You can find us at Saint John's Church on the corner of McCarty and Jefferson Streets."

Gavin smiled and said, "I can do that. I'll see you this coming Sunday, then. What time?"

"Come to eleven o'clock mass; then join us for lunch afterwards in the rectory," Aidan said.

"I will, thank you very much," Gavin said.

"Take care, lad," Finnegan said, tipping is wide-brimmed black hat.

Aiden whipped the horses and said, "Move along."

The wagon lurched forward then slowly moved away.

Gavin watched them until they made a turn and were out of sight. He looked back at the front entrance of the printing house and headed for the door. He turned the handle and opened the door. Inside, he found several men working behind desks. They were all middle-aged and wore visors and spectacles. "Good day, gentlemen, I'm here to see a Mr. Fitzpatrick."

A man raised his hand and said, "That would be me."

Gavin made for him with purpose and stopped just inches from his desk. "My name is Gavin Gilroy. I'm here about the apprenticeship."

The man removed his glasses and stared at Gavin strangely. "You're who?"

"Gavin Gilroy. We corresponded last month. I don't have the letter anymore, but you said you were looking forward to my arrival for the position."

"Wait, you must have corresponded with the other Mr. Fitzpatrick, my brother, Elmer. He's in the back; he runs the operations of our printing house," the man said, standing up and motioning for Gavin to follow. He opened a set of double doors and went into a large open space full of unusual and loud equipment. "Elmer!"

A hand waved from the far side of a machine followed by a shout. "Over here, Edwin."

"He's there; go talk to him," Edwin said then turned and left Gavin standing alone on the printing floor.

Gavin briskly walked to where he'd seen the hand wave, to find a man who looked very similar to Fitzpatrick covered in black ink and working on a machine. "Mr. Fitzpatrick, my name is Gavin Gilroy. I'm here about the apprenticeship."

"You're prompt, aren't you?" Elmer said, not looking up.

"Yes, sir, I'm ready to get to work," Gavin said, excited.

Elmer stopped working and stood up. He eyed Gavin up and down and asked, "Where are your things?"

"I don't have any, sir," Gavin said, feeling embarrassed by his response.

"You don't have a change of clothes or shoes? You do realize you'll be covered from head to toe in ink, don't you?" Elmer said.

"Sir, I sorta lost my things along the trip. It's a long story," Gavin lied.

Elmer raised his hand. "No matter, I have an extra set of clothes you can have. They belonged to the last apprentice. He up and quit without notice. It's hard to find good help around here."

"Thank you, sir."

"I suppose you'll want to eat and rest," Elmer said.

Standing at attention, Gavin said, "Sir, I'm ready to get to work."

Elmer nodded, glad to hear Gavin's response. "Good, let's get you those clothes and show you around."

CHAPTER FOUR

JEFFERSON CITY, MISSOURI

APRIL 10, 1891

Anna opened her eyes to find her parents standing above her. "Am I dreaming?"

Clara took Anna's hand, kissed it, and then began to sob. "Oh, my precious little Anna."

Edward came to the other side of the bed and took Anna's other hand. "How are you feeling?"

"Tired and my side hurts," Anna replied. She glanced past her mother and saw a man wearing a white coat, no doubt a doctor, and a woman dressed like a cowboy. "Who's that?"

Edward smiled and said, "That's Abigail. She's here to help find your sister Emma."

"Is she a policeman or marshal?" Anna asked.

"No, she's a bounty hunter," Edward said. "Honey, can you tell us anything about who took you or where your sister might be?"

"Can't we find a better time to ask these questions?" Clara asked.

"The sooner we can find Emma, the better," Edward said.

"The poor thing just woke. She's exhausted, she's been shot, and her shoulder is badly injured; she needs rest," Clara declared.

"And who's that?" Anna said, pointing at Milton.

"He's with the Pinkerton Detective Agency. He's also here to help find Emma," Edward said.

"Why don't you sit and rest. I'll get all of these people out of here," Clara said.

Anna gently squeezed Clara's hand and said, "Mother, it's fine. I escaped just so I could find help and get Emma rescued."

"Are you sure?" Clara asked.

"I'm positive. Emma needs our help, and I'll do whatever I can to save her," Anna answered.

Abigail took a step closer to Anna so she could hear.

Anna faced Edward and said, "We were taken first by a barge down the Kansas River. We disembarked and were then sold. I believe we were in Kansas City. We then were sold again, placed on a train, and ended up here. I escaped and ran."

"Can you describe the men who brought you to Jefferson City?" Edward asked.

"Yes, they had French names and accents," Anna replied.

"What were their names?" Abigail asked, taking a couple of steps closer.

"Francois and Jacques, that's all I remember," Anna said.

"Were these the men who took you first?" Edward asked.

"No, another man by the name of Albert took us," Anna said.

"Could you describe any of them well enough that

someone could draw a sketch?" Abigail asked.

"I think so," Anna answered.

Abigail walked up to Edward and said, "We need to find a sketch artist in town. Do you know where we might start?"

"No, but I'll find out," Edward said, jumping to his feet.

"We can help with that. I'll have Harrison look into it," Milton said.

"Very well," Edward said, sitting back down.

Abigail walked up to the edge of the bed and asked, "I'm sorry about what happened to you, but believe me when I say that I'll do whatever it takes to find your sister, I swear it."

"Thank you," Anna said.

Abigail took out a notebook and pencil from a vest pocket and handed it to Anna. "I need you to write down every detail. Try to put your thoughts into chronological order from the first time you encountered Albert until your escape. Don't leave out any detail. You never know what might be important."

Anna opened the small notebook and thumbed until she found a blank page. Looking up at Abigail, she asked, "Why do people do such things?"

"People can be cruel and violent," Abigail said.

"Violence and violent men are abhorrent and must be done away with," Clara said.

"Violence is just a way of the world, has been and always will be. Men that peddle in violence will always be around. That's why we must counter their violence with our own."

Nodding, Clara said, "I know you're right. I just wish it didn't have to be that way."

"I couldn't agree more, ma'am, but until that day comes, those of us like me will be here to fight and defend those who can't," Abigail said.

"Thank you," Clara said.

"Now, Anna, write down every detail, and get it to me as soon as you can," Abigail said, giving Anna a big smile. "I'll let you do that and get some rest too." Abigail turned and readied to leave.

"Miss Abigail," Anna said.

Turning back around, Abigail asked, "Yes."

"There's a detail that you should know about. The French men said something about Baron. I believe it's a person."

"Baron?" Abigail asked.

"Yes, I don't know who it refers to," Anna replied. "He only said Baron was going to love us."

Clara gasped. "Oh, dear God, I think I'm going to be ill."

Abigail nodded. "Thank you, Anna, I'll look into it."

"I'll let you know when I'm done writing down my notes," Anna said.

"Anna, you're a brave and strong girl, I want you to know that."

"Thank you, but I'll do anything for my sister, anything," Anna said.

"We'll get her back," Abigail said. As she went to leave, Milton stopped her.

"Can we talk outside?" Milton asked.

"Of course," Abigail said.

Exiting the room, Milton pulled Harrison aside and gave him instructions to go find out about a sketch artist.

"Anything?" Dwight asked, leaning up against the wall, chewing on a match.

"Yeah, she mentioned hearing something about someone called Baron," Abigail said.

"That does give us something to go on," Dwight said.

"I also gave her a notebook. She'll jot everything down, and Harrison is getting a sketch artist so we can put some faces to their names. I want to know what these men look like."

"Good idea," Dwight said.

"How about we go see what we can find out about who Baron is?" Abigail said.

"Can I join you?" Milton asked. "We can chat more about this along the way."

"I'm fine with it," Dwight said.

"Sure, you can tag along," Abigail said.

"Time to go hit up the local watering holes," Dwight quipped.

"We're going to bars?" Milton asked. "We should go talk to the local sheriff or police chief, see if he knows any Baron."

"Not a bad idea, how about you do that, then?" Abigail said. "We've come to find that drunks tend to know a lot, and the liquor makes the information flow easier."

"Makes sense; then to the bars we go," Milton said.

***

Abigail, Dwight and Milton spent the next four hours going from one bar to the next. The only information they gathered in reference to someone named Baron was met with either silence or ignorance. It appeared the people who knew who it was were not willing to speak, and that could only mean they feared for their lives. Whoever Baron was, he was powerful. This led the group to finally go to the sheriff. If someone could put such fear in the locals, he was certainly known to the law.

Milton entered the sheriff's office first to find Harrison there already. "I didn't expect to see you here," Milton said to Harrison, who was sitting casually talking to a bearded man at a desk.

"I was able to get a sketch artist," Harrison said.

"Oh, good," Milton said.

Abigail and Dwight walked in behind Milton.

She looked around and noticed it seemed like every other sheriff's office she'd ever been in. A few desks, gun racks and several jail cells.

"Who's your friend, Ulysses?" the bearded man asked.

"That man there is my partner, his name is Milton Wallace, and those two are bounty hunters hired by the esteemed Mr. Fulton," Harrison answered.

"Bounty hunters, huh?" the bearded man sneered.

It was apparent to Abigail and Dwight that the man,

who they suspected was the sheriff, didn't care for their types.

"I'm Sheriff Barlow. I'll admit right from the start that the case involving Anna Fulton's shooting is a local case and we're heading it up, so if you have any information, I suggest you share it with us," Barlow said.

"Sheriff, not to step on toes, but this case is now an interstate matter, as her abduction occurred in Kansas," Milton said. "We've been hired, and as you know, the Pinkerton Detective Agency has been granted a lot of leeway when investigating cases. We have come to expect the local law to help us in a reciprocal matter. We're not here to step on toes but help each other."

"I know you Pinkerton types. You like to barge into towns like this and bully your way around. I'm only being nice…"

"This is nice?" Abigail joked.

"Mind your matters, little lady," Barlow snapped. "I'll say it once, I'm only being nice because me and Ulysses here go way back."

Milton smiled and stepped up to the desk. He removed his hat and took a seat next to Harrison. "Now that we've gotten all the introductions and parameters of our relationship out of the way, let me ask you if you happen to know a person who goes by the name Baron."

Barlow froze. He leaned back, spit into a spittoon and answered, "Never heard of a Baron. Is he some sort of royalty? I seem to recall we kicked those bastards out of here during the Revolutionary War."

"The girl Anna said that name was mentioned several

times. We've been to numerous bars asking around, and everyone seems quiet when asked. It appears this person exists but has everyone fearful to speak out. I figured any person with that influence would be known by the local law, and that would be you."

"Like I said, never heard of a Baron," Barlow said.

Milton looked at Harrison then to Abigail and Dwight. He put his focus back on Barlow and said, "Whoever he is, he must be powerful, and guess what, Sheriff, we'll find him." Milton realized he wasn't getting anywhere with the sheriff. He stood, nodded to Abigail and Dwight, and said, "Let's keep asking around. Someone is bound to tell us."

"Ulysses, I suggest you keep your partner under control. This is my town, not his," Barlow warned.

Harrison stood, donned his hat and replied, "Nice seeing you again."

Barlow nodded then spit again, his hands folded on his belly.

The group exited the office.

Abigail walked up to Milton and said, "Something is going on, and it appears it runs deep."

"I think you're right," Milton said. "I think I'm going to send a telegram to Chicago letting them know. We might need some additional support."

"I'll go do it," Harrison offered.

"You sure?" Milton asked.

"It's a menial task, perfect for a new employee like myself," Harrison said.

"Okay, do that and meet us at that saloon there,"

Milton said.

Harrison nodded and strutted off.

Abigail watched Harrison walk off. There was something she didn't trust about him. Maybe it was because he didn't talk much or the way he looked at her. All she knew was she felt like her guard went up around him.

"I have a different idea," Dwight said. "I think we're going about this wrong."

"What do you suggest?" Milton asked.

"We don't ask for Baron, we ask about where we can find some young girls to spend time with," Dwight said.

The suggestion sounded despicable, but it could work, Abigail thought.

"Then we need to go to the brothels instead," Milton said.

"Yep, and there's one right there," Dwight said, pointing at a large Victorian house at the end of the street.

"How do you know that's a brothel? I don't see any signage," Milton asked.

"Let's just say Dwight here has a nose for finding such establishments," Abigail said. "You two go find out what you can. I'll go to this saloon and wait for Harrison; I'll keep asking around."

Milton and Dwight tipped their hats and headed towards the brothel.

Abigail could sense this job was taking an odd turn for the worse. Something sinister was lurking in this town, and she wouldn't rest until she exposed it.

***

Like before, Abigail left the bar with no information. She had waited for Harrison, but he never arrived. Tired and in need of sleep, she made her way to the hotel where they were staying and went to her room.

Just as she was getting undressed, someone knocked at the door.

"Yes," Abigail said.

"It's me, Dwight."

Abigail unlocked the door and opened it to find Dwight and Milton standing there. "Anything?"

Dwight pushed the door open and came in, followed by Milton. "We think we found it. This is the place," Dwight said, taking out a piece of paper and showing it to her.

Abigail took the paper and read it. "Clayton House."

"Yes, that's where we can go and get, quote unquote, young girls. This must be where they've taken them," Dwight said.

Abigail grabbed her gun belt, wrapped it around herself, and said, "Let's go."

A broad smile stretched across Dwight's face. "What's the plan of attack? Just go in there guns blazing?"

Abigail removed her Colt, half-cocked it and spun the cylinder. She gave Dwight a look and replied, "That's exactly what we're going to do."

"Wait, hold on. Where's Harrison?" Milton asked.

"Don't know, he never showed up at the saloon, and

we don't have time to waste," Abigail said.

"But we need to plan this," Milton said.

"We do have a plan. Kill everyone and save those kids," Dwight said.

"No, wait, we don't know if this is where Emma is being held. We don't know anything about this Clayton House. We can't go in there and just start killing people," Milton said.

"I hate to say it, but he's got a point," Abigail said.

"Then what do we do?" Dwight asked.

"We watch it, see who's coming and going. We find someone who's been there and question them," Milton said. "Once we have a confirmation, then we go in."

"Okay," Abigail said.

"Why not just try to go in as if we're a customer?" Dwight asked.

"On account that I think it's not that easy; you'll be scrutinized. No, we sit and wait, catch someone and question them," Milton said.

"We agree; let's go," Abigail said, anxious to get going.

Banging on the door startled them.

"Yeah!" Abigail hollered.

"It's Harrison. Open up."

Abigail opened the door, and there stood Harrison with his usual stoic stare. "Where have you been?" she asked.

"Good question. Where were you?" Milton asked.

"At the telegram office. I started asking around; it led me to another saloon. I asked around and got nothing," he answered. "Have you found something out?"

"We have, a place called Clayton House. It's a place where men can meet young girls," Dwight said.

"You think this place is it?" Harrison asked.

"Possibly," Milton replied. "We're headed out now to scout the location."

"Okay," Harrison said.

The group walked out the door and into Fisk, who was returning from a late dinner.

"Hello all," Fisk said, his slurred speech indicating he'd had more than a few drinks.

The group nodded and passed him, with only Abigail saying hello back.

"Where are you off to in such a hurry?" Fisk asked. "Oh, wait, do you have a clue? Can you tell me?" he continued, now following them down the stairs.

Abigail stopped near the bottom of the stairwell, turned and said, "Go to bed. If we have something to tell you, we'll come to you."

"Very well, I wish you luck," Fisk said, appearing wounded by her comment.

"Don't worry, I'll fulfill my promise. You'll have a great article to write," she said and rushed off to catch the others.

***

Gavin finished his official first full day with the Clancy Printing House, and it was definitely hard work. After working on his parents' farm for his entire life, he didn't imagine something could be physically harder, but working in a printing house was just that.

Elmer had him doing everything from hauling barrels of ink, mopping the floor, cleaning racks, fetching lunch, swabbing the toilet area—yes, they had a toilet inside. It was a surprise to see and convenient, but the smell was horrendous. He hadn't learned much about operating a printing press, but he knew that would eventually come. If he was one thing, it was a hard worker, and he also knew that it would not only take hard work but time, so he vowed to remain patient.

Elmer left him for the day with a basket of food and a half-full pitcher of beer. He said there was also a surprise in the basket, which he discovered was pipe tobacco. He'd never smoked, but tonight he'd give it a try. He took a chair from the front office and set it out on the walkway near the entrance. He dove into the food first and washed it all down with the beer. In the matter of a few days he'd had alcohol twice. He was truly living the life of a man now. When he was finished with his meal, he put the tobacco in a pipe that Elmer had provided and, using a match, lit the bowl. Of course, never having smoked before, he choked the first time, not knowing that he shouldn't inhale the smoke. Once he became comfortable, he leaned back and puffed on the pipe, blowing the smoke out and admiring the rich cherry smell of it.

On the street he watched as people walked by, many waving and saying hello. Life was truly good for him. He wasn't sure what else was coming his way, but he felt very confident that the days ahead would be filled with great things for him.

His work schedule wasn't a surprise. He was supposed to work twelve hours a day, from five in the morning until five in the afternoon, and do this six days per week, Monday through Saturday with Sunday off, although he was required to ensure the toilet and front office were presentable for use by Monday morning. He had thought there would be other apprentices, but to his surprise, he was it. He sort of enjoyed the privacy of the building and his quarters, which were quite large. Being that he worked for a printing house, he didn't have a shortage of things to read. Elmer and his brother, the owners, kept a copy of everything they printed and stored them in a back office. Elmer gave him permission to read anything he wanted, and that overjoyed him.

With the pipe empty and the streetlights on, Gavin picked up the basket and called it a night. He went to the back office, found a book, and proceeded to his quarters, where he'd read until he fell asleep.

CHAPTER FIVE

JEFFERSON CITY, MISSOURI

APRIL 11, 1891

In order to cover more area, the group divided in two, with Dwight and Abigail taking the right side of the street outside Clayton House, a two-story house across the street from the capitol building in downtown Jefferson City.

With no moon and only a few gaslight streetlamps, it was hard to see. The house itself was also darkened. They could see a few candles or oil lamps illuminated inside, but hadn't, after three hours, seen one person enter or exit the house.

"Someone has to come soon, don't you think?" Dwight asked.

Ignoring his question, Abigail asked Dwight something that had been concerning her since meeting Milton and Harrison. "Do you trust those two?"

"Of course not," Dwight replied.

"I know we're always skeptical, but I don't trust that Harrison fella. He's up to no good, I just know it," Abigail said.

"He is a bit quiet, isn't he?" Dwight said. "He stands around and stares most of the time. I wonder what's going through his mind."

"Probably thinking about how he's going to kill us,"

Abigail joked.

The two laughed.

"I haven't asked you, but how are you doing?" Dwight asked.

"What does that mean?" Abigail asked.

"I can't help but notice you're different since Madeleine went to live with that family in Dallas," Dwight said, referring to the girl Abigail had saved from an abusive family three years before. Abigail had tried to make the situation work by going to visit her often after a job, but soon it became apparent that Madeleine needed a more stable upbringing.

"I'm fine," she snorted.

"You're not; you're different," Dwight said.

"Different how?" she asked.

"You're mean now; you weren't like that before. You'd take care of business on a job, but you were never openly mean to average people; but now you're as mean as a dog who's had his food taken away from him."

"I'm not mean," Abigail said, defending herself.

"Yes, you are. You bite people's heads off just for saying good morning," Dwight said.

"Do we have to talk about this now?" she asked, growing annoyed.

"I'd like to, yes; we're partners and I want the old Abby back," Dwight said.

"Well, she's gone, okay. She grew up and realized that the world is just…just…"

"Just what?" he asked.

"Cruel, it's damn cruel," she blurted out.

"Of course it is. It's always been, but you seemed to rise above it. You were always optimistic. You saw the world for what it was, but it didn't change you. The second you let Madeleine go, you've been…"

"Enough, I don't want to talk about this," she snapped.

"We can go visit her when we're done here. How does that sound?" Dwight asked.

"No."

"Why not?"

"On account she needs to forget about me. She's better off without me, and that's that," Abigail scoffed.

"Hell no, she isn't, and you think she'll forget you. Woman, because of you that little girl has a chance in life, hell, she has a life. Who knows where the abuse she was suffering would have gone. Someone can't forget that and especially can't forget the person who saved them from it. That little girl needs you in her life even if it's only every so often."

Abigail stewed on his comment. Deep down she wanted nothing else than to see Madeleine, but she did feel her brief visits weren't good for her or Madeleine. After meeting a nice family after a job in Dallas, she had them watch her while she'd go away. Soon she came to see that Madeleine needed to be with them full-time and her out of the way.

"What do you say?" Dwight asked.

"No, I'm not going to Dallas to see her, not after this job, not after the next, never," she growled.

"You're being a damn fool. That little girl loves you

and needs you, even if you only visit once per year."

"Can we stop talking and focus on the job here?" she asked.

He looked around and said, "Like there's a lot going on."

"Are you dim-witted? I don't want to talk about it, and maybe I'm a mean old bitch now 'cause my partner is a jackass and makes my life difficult," she barked.

"Just trying to help. I miss the old Abby," he said.

"Like I said, she's gone. Deal with it," she said.

"Your words are like daggers, I swear; you know I'd do anything for you. I'd take a bullet for you, and you think the best way to show me respect is with your sharp tongue," Dwight said, his tone indicating how hurt he was.

Abigail shook her head. He was right, but she refused to let his words affect her. When she last saw Madeleine, she had told her it was the last time and said goodbye. Madeleine had pleaded with her to come back and see her, but she kept telling her it was for her own good. She wasn't sure if she'd ever get over letting Madeleine go, but no matter what anyone said, she'd always believe it was truly the best decision.

A horse and rider trotted past, stopping in front of Clayton House. A shadowy figure dismounted and walked to the front door. There his identity was exposed by the yellow glow of a gas lamp. It was Sheriff Barlow.

"Are my eyes deceiving me, or is that the good sheriff going in there?" Dwight asked.

"I knew that son of a bitch was up to no good,"

Abigail snorted.

"What now?" Dwight asked.

"We wait until he leaves, then get him to answer some of our questions," Abigail said.

"I'm going to go tell those two what we're going to do so we have a coordinated plan," Dwight said and ran across the street.

Moments later, Dwight returned with Harrison and Milton following.

"We're not in agreement on what to do," Dwight said.

"What's the problem?" Abigail asked.

Harrison stepped up and answered her question, his hands on his hips. "We need to be careful. Sheriff Barlow is a popular figure in town. If we do this wrong, we could end up head deep in trouble and destroy any chance we have of finding the girl."

"But he's in there doing God knows what. He needs to answer some questions," Abigail said, challenging Harrison.

"He has some good points. We don't know what's happening in there. I agree on the idea of questioning someone coming out of there, but the sheriff could land us in some trouble if we're wrong," Milton said.

"I won't go along with nabbing the sheriff and forcing him to talk. I won't do it without more concrete evidence," Harrison declared.

"Again I agree with my partner. What if the information we received was faulty? We're making an assumption it's accurate, and if we were so sure, why not just go in there forcibly?" Milton asked.

Abigail pulled her pistol and said, "Then let's do that."

"Abby, they've made some valid points," Dwight said, touching her arm. He motioned with his head for her to reholster the pistol.

"You're siding with them?" she asked.

"I am, but only because they're right," Dwight said.

Dwight's shift shocked Abigail. "Then how do you propose we find out what's happening in there?"

"I like the plan but not holding up the sheriff. That could easily go off the rails," he answered.

"We could try to enter as clientele," Harrison suggested.

"That could work, but it could also backfire," Milton said. "If we see the sheriff in there, he knows us all."

"We're standing around while there's a real possibility that Emma and other children are being abused in there right now. I'm done talking; it's time to do something," Abigail snapped.

The group turned silent.

"It's time to go in there and find out what's going on," Abigail said and started towards Clayton House, her pistol in her grip.

"Abby, hold up!" Dwight called out to her.

"Stop her before this gets real ugly," Harrison warned.

"Abigail, don't do it!" Milton hollered.

She was done talking. She needed to know if Emma was in there.

Harrison took off after her. He got in front of her and put out his hand, stopping her advance. "You're not going in there."

She looked at his hand then at him and said, "Get out of my way."

"No, you're making a mistake," Harrison said.

Dwight and Milton ran up and immediately tried to lower the tension.

"You and I don't agree on how to proceed. If you don't wish to go inside, you don't have to, but I'm going in there," Abigail said.

"Abby, calm down," Dwight said.

"Listen to your partner," Harrison said.

"I've never seen you this way. You're being a coward," Abigail snapped.

Taken aback by her sharp response, he fired off a few of his own. "You might think I'm a coward, but I'm not a damn fool. You claim you want to save these children, but you have zero evidence of what's going on in there. What if you're wrong? What if you go in there and it's not what we've been told. You have to remember only one person told us, that's it. You and I both know how unreliable people can be."

"I'm going in, and there's nothing anyone can do to stop me," she said, sidestepping Harrison.

Harrison pulled his pistol, cocked it, and placed the muzzle near her head. "Stand down."

She stopped, frozen to the spot. Hearing the hammer on his pistol go back sent both shivers of fear and anger. She turned her head and glared at him. "You're going to shoot me?"

"Put your pistol down," Milton pleaded with Harrison.

Harrison wasn't listening to anyone. He returned Abigail's glare with his own. His index finger rested on the trigger, but he wasn't applying any pressure…yet. "Stand down or I'll put you down."

Dwight ripped his pistol from his holster, cocked it back and aimed at Harrison. "You shoot her, you die."

Dwight's response forced Milton to act but not before Dwight pulled his second pistol and aimed it at Milton. "Don't try it. Tell your friend to lower his iron or I'll end him right here."

"Damn it, people, we're on the same side here," Milton crowed.

The front door of Clayton House opened, and out stepped Barlow. The light from the streetlamps allowed him to see the standoff feet from him. "What the hell is going on out here?"

Not afraid, Abigail shouted, "What are you doing in there, Sheriff?"

Barlow laughed and replied, "I was just visiting a lady friend."

"How old is your friend?" she asked.

"Don't blame me for what's about to happen," Harrison said.

Barlow stepped off the walkway and strutted towards them, his right hand dangling near his pistol.

Abigail could feel the cold steel of the muzzle pointed at her head but kept her focus on Barlow's advance.

"Is this some sort of Mexican standoff?" Barlow joked.

"What were you doing in there, Sheriff?" Abigail again asked.

"I told you I was enjoying some time with a lady friend," Barlow answered, walking up to within a couple of feet of her. "It doesn't look like any of you will win this situation except for the handsome fella there," he said, referring to Dwight. "You, sweetheart, will most certainly end up with a round through that pretty head of yours."

"I want to meet your friend," Abigail said.

Barlow laughed and asked, "You want to meet my friend? Why, you think I'm doing something I'm not supposed to do?"

"Yes," Abigail replied.

Barlow spit on the ground and said, "I can assure you that your suspicions are false. We've been trying to keep our relationship discreet; you know how people talk."

"I want to meet her," Abigail insisted.

Barlow spit and said, "Then come on, let's go visit my friend."

Harrison lowered his pistol and holstered it.

Dwight followed suit.

"Follow me," Barlow said, spinning around and heading towards the front door.

Abigail was right behind him, with the others close behind.

Barlow knocked on the door and gave Abigail a toothy smile. "My friend won't like being bothered."

Abigail didn't reply. She kept her eye on Barlow and on the windows to either side of the door. Her senses were heightened, telling her that something bad was about to happen.

"If you're wrong, you're through, your career is over," Harrison barked.

"Who is it?" a man hollered from the other side of the door.

"It's Sheriff Barlow. There's an uninvited guest out here," Barlow hollered.

"I thought you said your friend was a woman," Abigail said.

The curtain moved, catching Dwight's attention. He looked and saw a man holding a double-barreled shotgun. "Abby, step away from the door!" He shoved her away just as the door opened. A man stood in the open space, the shotgun in his shoulder. He aimed it at Dwight and pulled the trigger. Both barrels blasted and struck Dwight in the chest. The force from the blast threw him from the walkway to the street below.

Still holding her pistol, she leveled it at the man, who was now frantically reloading, and she pulled the trigger. Her shot hit him square in the chest, knocking him down.

Barlow drew, but she was on him fast, pivoting and taking another shot, this one hitting Barlow in the throat. He clenched the open wound and gagged. She cocked the pistol again and finished him off with a shot to the head.

Harrison and Milton stood in awe at her speed and

agility.

She raced to Dwight's side, but he was dead. The twin blasts from the shotgun had killed him instantly. Angry, she got up and ran inside.

Milton and Harrison followed, their pistols drawn now.

Abigail quickly surveyed the candlelit foyer and hallway but didn't see anyone. A long stairwell on her right led to the second floor. She raced up the stairs and looked down the hallway. On the wall, four candle sconces illuminated the space. Four doors, two on either side, sat closed. With her pistol out in front of her, she marched down the hall.

The first door on the right opened, and out stepped a half-naked man. "What's the commotion?"

She answered his question with a bullet.

The man dropped to his knees and fell over dead.

She reached the now open doorway and looked inside the room. In the orange glow of the lantern, a young girl was huddled up on the bed, her legs pulled in tight. "Emma?" she asked.

The girl shook her head. "Help me."

"That's what I'm here to do," she said. "Is there anyone else in the house you're aware of?"

The girl nodded.

Milton and Harrison appeared. They looked at the girl and both sighed.

"You were right," Harrison said.

"You're damn right I was," she said, pushing past him and heading for the second door, only to find it locked. She stepped back and kicked it, her foot landing just to the side of the knob. The door exploded inward. She raced in and saw a man getting dressed. In the bed, like before, another girl, this one younger, lay in the fetal position crying. Abigail cocked her pistol and shot the man through the head.

Milton ran into the room and went to the girl. "Come, we're here to save you."

Abigail proceeded out and went to the third door. This time it was unlocked. She opened it to find a man pointing a pistol at her. He fired but missed, the round striking just to her right and shattering part of the doorjamb, sending fragments of wood and splinters everywhere. She aimed and shot the man before he could cock and fire again. Like usual, her aim was true. The man reeled backwards and fell onto the bed, dead.

"Are you Emma?" Abigail asked.

The girl pointed to the last closed door in the hallway.

Abigail ran out and kicked the door in to find a lone girl sitting on the bed.

"Emma?" Abigail asked.

"Did my sister send you?" Emma asked.

"Yes," Abigail said, scooping her up in her arms and heading back out the door. "Has anyone touched you in an inappropriate way?"

She shook her head no.

In the hallway, Milton and Harrison had gathered the other children.

"Is that her?" Milton asked.

"Yeah," Abigail said.

"You did it, unbelievable," Milton said.

"Stop talking. Let's get these children out of here," she said, racing past him and down the stairs.

***

Gavin woke to the sound of gunfire. He blinked repeatedly, hoping his eyes would adjust to the dim light, but they didn't. He turned the oil lantern up and headed to a window that overlooked an alleyway between the printing office and another commercial building. He looked down but couldn't see a thing.

Curious as to where the gunfire was coming from, he headed down into the printing floor and outside through the front office. He heard voices talking down the street. He looked and saw a group of people; he wasn't sure how many there were but roughly counted three adults and three children. He rubbed his eyes to clear them and squinted to get a better view.

"Is that a…?" he asked out loud to himself.

"What are you looking at?" Abigail barked at him, her arms draped over Emma.

"Ah, no, sorry, I heard some gunshots is all. Is everything okay?" Gavin asked.

"Mind your own business and get back inside," Abigail ordered.

Not wanting to get into trouble, Gavin rushed back inside but not before positively identifying Abigail under the glow of a street gas lamp and that what he did see down the street was a body.

Back inside the front office, he locked the door. His heart was thumping; a tinge of fear ran up his spine but so did a tinge of excitement. He couldn't say he'd witnessed his first gunfight, but he could with confidence say he'd seen the aftermath of one.

Happy in his new life experience, he made his way back to his quarters and went to bed.

***

Edward stepped away from Emma's bedside and walked up to Abigail, who stood hovering in the corner like a guardian angel. "I owe you so much," he said.

"I'm just happy we found her and as quickly as we did," Abigail said. "And I'm happy that she wasn't touched in that manner."

"Me too, but this entire ordeal is very traumatic," he replied. "Your partner, I'm very sorry. Just let me know what I can do. I'll pay for all the burial and transportation expenses so he can be interred with his family," Edward said.

"He didn't have family," she said.

"Sorry to hear that. Just let me know what I can do; I'll do anything. I owe him, you and the Pinkertons so much," he said.

Emma looked up from the bed and said, "There are others."

"What did you say?" Abigail asked, coming closer.

"Children, there are others. I was with others on the

train. They only took four of us there; the others went somewhere else," Emma said.

"Where?" Abigail asked.

"I don't know for sure," Emma answered.

"Can we please, for the sake of God, not talk about this?" Clara blared.

"But if there are other children in harm's way, we must do something," Abigail said.

"I agree with Abigail," Edward said then faced Clara and continued, "We'd want the same if it were our child still out there."

Clara thought for a moment and relented. "You're right."

Abigail approached the bed and asked, "Can you recall anything at all that might lead us to the other children?"

"No," Emma answered.

"Anna mentioned the name Baron. Does that ring a bell?" Abigail asked.

Emma thought for a few seconds then said, "Yes, I do remember that name being said."

"But nothing else?" Abigail asked.

"No, I can't, I'm sorry," Emma said, feeling bad that she couldn't recall.

"Can we now give her some time to rest?" Clara asked.

Seeing Emma was getting frustrated about her lack of clarity, Abigail replied, "It's probably a good idea to let her rest."

"Sorry," Emma said.

"Don't apologize; you've been through a lot," Abigail said and exited the room promptly.

"I'll walk you out," Edward said, exiting with Abigail. When the door was closed, he pulled her aside. I have deposited some money for you and Dwight, God rest his soul, in an account under your name at the Missouri Bank and Trust. It covers everything; plus, I didn't want to tell you in earshot of my wife, didn't think talking business was appropriate."

"Thank you," Abigail said.

Farther down the hallway, Milton sat in a chair, whittling a piece of wood with a knife. He glanced up at them and nodded.

"I best get back inside," Edward said and disappeared back into the hospital room.

"Well? Anything?" Milton hollered from down the hall.

Abigail walked to him and said, "She does recall the name Baron being used, but she can't remember anything else."

"We had Dwight's body taken to the undertaker," Milton said, pocketing his knife and setting the piece of wood on the floor.

"Thank you," Abigail said with a somber tone. "Where's your partner?"

"I sent Harrison to the telegraph office to see if anything has come in from Chicago and to let them know we found the Fulton girls."

"Okay," Abigail said.

"I suppose our work is done," Milton said.

"We found Emma, but I won't rest until I find the other children and whoever this Baron is," Abigail declared.

"You're going to keep looking?" Milton asked.

"I can't in good conscience move on knowing other children are being abused," Abigail answered.

"Unfortunately, we can't join in," Milton said. "Our job is done. We'll need to head back to Chicago, in the morning probably. Otherwise I'd join you on this crusade."

"That's okay. I can handle myself," Abigail said. "It was nice meeting you."

Milton stood and said, "Before you go, I want to say what you did back at that house was nothing but exceptional. Your reputation doesn't do you justice. If you ever think about getting out of bounty hunting and want a career with the Pinkertons, send me a wire."

"I will," Abigail said and walked off.

Harrison appeared in the hallway with another man and walked up to Abigail. "I want to express my condolences for your partner," Harrison said.

She hadn't forgotten his treatment and never would. "I won't accept your apology. And in some ways I hold you a bit responsible for his death."

"That wasn't my fault," Harrison said.

"Excuse me, I don't wish to interrupt your disagreement, but I'm here to see Mr. and Mrs. Fulton," one of the other men said.

"Who are you?" Abigail asked.

"I'm Governor Strauss, a friend of Mr. and Mrs.

Fulton," Strauss said proudly.

"Friend? Where have you been all along, and why have you allowed this sort of business to happen in your capital city?" Abigail asked pointedly.

"Don't be rude," Harrison barked.

"I daresay, you are a callous one," Strauss said. He turned to Harrison and said, "Mr. Harrison, good to see you as always." He pushed past Abigail and strutted down the hallway, eventually going into Emma's hospital room.

As soon as he disappeared in the room, Abigail let Harrison have it. "If you hadn't forced the situation, we could have gotten the information we needed from the sheriff and gone into the house unannounced," Abigail snarled.

"I regret challenging you, but if you take a second to consider—"

Abigail held up her hand in a gesture for him to stop talking. "Silence."

"Don't tell me to be quiet," Harrison snapped.

"I just did. Now get out of my way," Abigail barked.

Harrison gave her a hard stare and wouldn't budge.

"Move or I'll make you move," she warned.

Harrison stepped to the side, giving her enough space to walk past.

"If I see you again, it will be too soon," Abigail said then walked off.

Harrison spit out a few choice words under his breath and headed towards Milton. "That woman has nerve."

"I do remember you pulled your pistol and had it

pointed at her head," Milton said.

"She's blaming me for Dwight's death," Harrison growled.

"Put her out of your mind. Any word from Chicago?"

"Nothing," Harrison said.

"I overheard what the governor said. You know him?" Milton asked.

"I know a lot of people," Harrison replied.

"Well, partner, our job is done; the girls have been reunited. How about we get a few too many drinks tonight?" Milton asked.

"I'll pass. I need to get some rest. I might even go back to the telegraph office again," Harrison said.

"You do that. I'll see you later at the hotel, then, and get your bags packed. I'm betting we're on the first train out of here," Milton said, patting Harrison on the shoulder.

***

Abigail pushed the exit door to the hospital open to find Fisk sitting on the front steps. He turned and saw her then jumped to his feet.

"Miss Abigail, what's the news?" he asked.

"Emma is safe," she answered.

Looking sheepish, Fisk said, "I heard about Dwight. I'm so very sorry. My condolences."

"I'm sorry too, but he died doing what he loved, if that's a consolation," Abigail said. Just uttering the words struck an emotional chord in her. She needed to go back to her hotel room and really process the loss of Dwight. It was something she hadn't had the time to do yet.

"I suppose it is," Fisk said.

"If you'll excuse me, my work isn't done yet," Abigail said.

"Miss Abigail, if you're going after Baron, I may have a way of finding who he might be," Fisk said.

Abigail stopped in her tracks. "How would you know I'm looking for him?"

"Let's just say I've gotten to know your persistence," Fisk said.

"You have me intrigued. How can you find Baron?" Abigail asked.

"By using the power of the newspaper," Fisk said with a smile.

"What does that mean?" she asked, curious.

"By placing an advertisement and a reward for information leading to his whereabouts," Fisk said.

Her eyes widened. "I'm not one to compliment, but that's brilliant."

"Why, thank you," he said, pretending to take a bow.

She reached into her vest pocket, pulled out a few coins, and offered them to him. "That should be enough, right?"

"I don't need your money. I'll take care of the cost," Fisk said, waving her hand away.

"Are you sure?"

"Positive, it would be my pleasure to find this brute," Fisk said, his face showing determination.

Abigail smiled.

"Is that a smile I see on your face?" he asked.

"Not one of joy but of knowing there are other people that wish to see justice done," she answered.

"I'll leave you be, then. I hope to see you in the morning," Fisk said. He pivoted sharply on his heel and headed down the street.

Abigail made her exit too. She was exhausted and needed some time to mentally and emotionally go over what had happened today. She knew with a good night's rest, she'd be ready to pursue Baron with vigor.

***

When the timing was right, Gavin told Elmer about his encounter in the early morning hours with Abigail and the others.

"I heard about it. They killed the sheriff," Elmer said.

"Oh, they did?" Gavin asked, shocked to hear the news.

"Yeah, word is spreading fast that some woman gunslinger and her partner killed the sheriff," Elmer said, then pointed to a stack of paper. "Bring that over here."

Gavin rushed to the paper and carried it over. "Should I have stopped them or something?"

Taking the paper, Elmer placed it on a press and secured it with a brace. "God no, if you see anyone pull a gun, you get away from them as fast as you can, you hear me. You don't stand around and chicken neck it. You know what happens to chickens when they stick their necks out, don't you?"

"They get them cut off," Gavin answered. "We had chickens on our farm. I used to cut their heads off, so I'm quite familiar."

"There you go, then; just stay away from trouble. I don't need you getting shot or anything like that, you hear me. You've been a good worker the few days you've been here. I don't need to go find a new apprentice anytime soon," Elmer said.

"Speaking of trouble, are there any drinking establishments you recommend I can go where I won't get into trouble?" Gavin asked. He'd always heard about saloons and bars, and now he could go visit one. It being a Saturday night and having no work the next day, he wanted to go.

"Boy, didn't we just talk about not getting into trouble," Elmer chastised.

"Sir, I'm eighteen, hardly a boy," Gavin said, defending himself slightly.

Elmer stopped what he was doing and placed his hand on Gavin's shoulder. "You never left your house before much less gone to another town, have you?"

"No, sir."

"Listen, there's a saloon down on High Street. Go out the front, go left, go about five blocks, turn right, then it's on the corner. It's called the Lazy Susan Saloon. I know the owner; I'll meet you there around seven tonight. That way you'll have your first saloon experience and be under the watchful eye of someone you can trust."

"You'll do that for me?" Gavin asked.

"Of course," Elmer said. "Now, go get me the box of letters and the sponge."

"Yes, sir," Gavin said and darted off to get what Elmer needed.

***

Abigail woke to find it was dark outside. She hadn't planned on sleeping the entire day, but she had. She rushed to the table, found her pocket watch, the very same one that Grant had given her, and checked the time. It was almost ten o'clock. She hadn't just slept the entire day but almost the entire evening. Annoyed with herself, she quickly washed up, got dressed, and headed out the door. She was hoping to find Fisk and see if he'd found any useful information.

In the lobby she ran into Milton relaxing with a drink in his hand. He lifted his head and asked, "How are you, Abby? Do you mind if I call you that?"

She could tell he was tipsy. "That's fine. Have you seen my reporter friend?"

"Ah, no, haven't seen him. Say, word has really gone through town. Apparently you and Dwight are being called murderers by some of the locals for killing a corrupt sheriff."

"Welcome to my world," Abigail said then remembered that Milton was supposed to head back to Chicago. "Weren't you leaving today?"

"No, change of plans. Mr. Fulton has continued our

employment. He wishes us to help you find Baron and bring an end to this child-abduction ring."

Abigail didn't want to admit it, but she was happy to hear that. "Good, let's go to work."

"Work? Now?" Milton asked, surprised.

"Yes, I need to find Fisk. He might have some information for us concerning the mysterious Baron," Abigail said.

Harrison stepped inside the lobby and approached them. His eyes were wide and it was apparent he seemed anxious.

"Where have you been all day?" Milton asked.

"I have some critical information," Harrison said.

"You do?" Milton asked.

"I've found a man who has information on where Baron and the other children are. We need to go meet him," Harrison said.

"You're serious?" Milton asked.

"I am. Now come, we need to meet him," Harrison urged, turned and exited the lobby as quickly as he had entered.

***

Harrison led them through the bustling streets until they reached a barn at the edge of town.

"We're meeting this person in there?" Abigail said, holding a lantern in her left hand.

"This is where he told me to meet him," Harrison said.

"Who is this person?" Abigail asked, suspicious.

"I met him at the telegraph office. After leaving, he approached me and said he had information on the Fulton girl abduction and Baron. He wouldn't meet in public, said he'd meet me here at eleven o'clock, then hurried off. I went looking for everyone but couldn't find anyone," Harrison explained.

"I was busy," Abigail lied, not wanting to admit she had been asleep all day. She was feeling uneasy about this last minute and surprise meeting.

"You looked for me? I've been at the hotel bar," Milton said. "I thought we decided we'd get back on the case first thing in the morning." This was his defense for being a bit inebriated.

"After we talked to Mr. Fulton about extending the job to find Baron, I went back to the telegraph office to send that telegram to Chicago. I ran into this man there," Harrison said.

"So where is he?" Abigail asked.

Annoyed by her tone, Harrison snapped, his face tense, "What's the matter? I think he's in the barn."

"So he's in the barn? Is something wrong?" Abigail asked, picking up on a growing unease within Harrison.

"Nothing is wrong. Now do we want to meet this man or not?" Harrison asked.

"Lead the way," Milton said, waving his arms towards the barn door.

Harrison walked into the barn first, his lantern illuminating the space and showing it was empty. "Hello."

Milton came in behind him with Abigail following

close behind with a second lantern.

"Looks like he didn't show," Milton said.

A creak sounded in the corner.

They all turned to see a man step out of the shadows with a rifle in his hands.

Seeing the weapon, Abigail went for her pistol.

More figures emerged from the darkened corners of the barn, all holding weapons.

Like Abigail, Milton reached for his pistol but not before a round struck him in the head.

Blood from the exit wound splattered on Abigail's face.

Milton dropped to the ground, dead.

Those two rounds ushered in a volley of gunfire, several hitting Milton's dead body and one striking Abigail in the right side and exiting out the back. She took aim and squeezed off a round, hitting one man. Seeing there was no winning this fight, Abigail tossed the lantern. It crashed onto the dirt floor and burst into flames, the oil catching a stable door and hay on fire.

It was enough of a distraction for her. She raced out the door and into the alleyway, but not before rounds struck just behind her.

"Get her!" Harrison hollered.

Hearing him utter those words told her all she needed to know. He was behind this ambush and no doubt a party to the entire conspiracy along with Baron.

Utilizing the cover of the moonless night, she ran as hard as her legs would take her up the alley and onto the main street. The first horse she saw, she untied it, jumped on its back, and kicked her heels into its ribs. "Yaw!" She slapped the reins against the sides of the horse, causing it to rear slightly before galloping away.

Behind her she could hear the others yelling and shooting. Fortunately for her the darkness concealed her retreat. The question now was where she should go. She thought about warning Edward so he could get his family to a safe place then thought about her own safety. Unable to just leave without letting Edward know what had happened, she rode to the hospital. She dismounted, grunting in pain as she went, and ran inside the dimly lit building.

A nurse met her in the hallway. "Stop, who goes there?"

"I need to find Edward Fulton. It's an emergency," she cried out.

"They're not here anymore. Both Fulton girls and the other children left the hospital an hour ago, and I haven't seen her father or mother," the nurse said.

"That's impossible. They weren't well enough to leave, any of them," Abigail barked.

"I'm sorry, but they aren't here, and I have to ask you to leave," the nurse warned.

"Where did they take them?" Abigail asked, clutching her side and grimacing in pain.

"I don't know. Now you must leave," the nurse said. She looked and noticed Abigail was bleeding. "Have you been shot?"

"Who took them?" Abigail yelled.

"I'm not in any position to tell you. Now, you must

leave the premises immediately!" the nurse bellowed.

Abigail ripped her Colt from her holster, cocked it, and placed it against the nurse's forehead. "Who took the girls?"

Terrified, the nurse stuttered, "I don't know."

"Was it Edward or Clara?" Abigail asked.

"No," the nurse cried.

"Where were they going?"

"I, I, um, I don't know. Please don't hurt me," the nurse whined.

Anger welled up inside Abigail. "Can you tell me anything that is useful?"

"There were three men; they had a carriage; that's all I know. Oh, and they said they worked for Mr. Fulton, but I didn't see him. I haven't seen him since this afternoon," she mumbled.

Abigail heard what sounded like water hitting the floor. She looked down and saw the woman was urinating on herself. "You let those girls get taken again. I should just shoot you right here for being stupid."

"I didn't know, I swear. How was I to know?" she cried.

Commotion sounded in the street. It was the men led by Harrison.

The nurse looked past Abigail and saw them illuminated by a streetlamp. Assuming they were looking for Abigail, she wailed, "Help, she's in here!"

"Damn you!" Abigail barked then smacked the woman on the top of the head with the butt of her Colt.

The nurse dropped to the floor, unconscious.

"In the hospital," Harrison hollered.

Knowing she couldn't run forever, Abigail decided she'd fight it out. She ran to an open doorway along the hall and hid in the shadows.

The first man raced inside.

Abigail took aim and fired. She struck him in the chest.

He grunted and toppled to the floor.

She cocked the pistol and held it out, pointed towards the open entrance.

Another man came rushing in.

She again fired, hitting him.

He too fell to the floor.

Once more she cocked the pistol and waited.

A third man came running in. This man was firing as he went but didn't have a target he was shooting at.

Remaining calm, Abigail aimed and squeezed the trigger.

The .45-caliber round struck him in the neck. He grabbed at the wound in his neck and wailed in pain.

Abigail cocked the pistol again, stepped from the shadows, and took aim on him. "Die, you son of a bitch." She squeezed the trigger. This time the round struck him in the face.

He hit the wall behind him and slid down. He was dead before hitting the floor.

She had gotten a rough count of the men in the barn. With these three down, she had two more, and that included Harrison.

She took cover in the doorway again, but no one else

came in. They had gotten wind of the ambush she had for them. Sensing she needed to now flee, she sprinted down the hall until she came to a back door. She carefully opened it to see that it was a narrow alleyway. Quietly she peeked out, but with barely any light, she couldn't tell if someone was hiding in wait for her like she had done to them. Her side was stinging and the blood kept flowing. She had to get somewhere fast, or she'd lose too much blood and pass out. "Go, Abigail, just go." Risking it all, she ran out into the alleyway but found it was vacant. She sprinted until she hit a street. She looked both ways but didn't see Harrison. Feeling it was safe, she walked out and headed towards the riverfront.

***

Feeling the numerous drinks, Gavin decided he best go home or else he might disappoint Elmer. "Mr. Fitzpatrick, I want to thank you for a wonderful evening. I've had the time of my life."

Patting him on the back, Elmer said, "I'm happy you did."

"I think I'm going to go back to the shop," Gavin said.

"Good idea. Do you think you can find your way back?" Elmer asked.

"Yes, sir," Gavin said.

"Good, I'm going to stay here and have a few more. You have a great day off tomorrow," Elmer said.

"I will. I plan on going to church. I met a couple of

priests, really nice gentlemen. I'm not Catholic, but I promised I'd go to mass because—"

Elmer patted him on the shoulder and said, "You're drunk, and now you're talking too much. Go back to the shop and sleep it off. I'll see you Monday morning."

"Yes, sir," Gavin said, standing at attention.

"I feel when you stand like that you're about to salute me or something," Elmer joked.

Gavin slouched slightly and said, "My father always told me to stand tall."

"You're fine. Now go, and be careful," Elmer said, pushing him out the saloon doors.

Outside, Gavin looked up and down the streets. He mumbled to himself the directions to the shop. "Take a right, go to—wait, was it…um, yes, it's down there, then left and go five blocks and the shop will be on the right-hand side. Yep, that's it."

Not looking, he walked into Abigail, who was stumbling too.

"I'm sorry, excuse me," Gavin said.

Abigail shoved him out of the way but lost her footing and fell to the ground hard. She grunted in pain and tried to get up but was having a difficult time.

"Oh no, I knocked you down. I'm so sorry. I never really drank before," Gavin said, offering to help her up.

She batted his hand away and snapped, "Get away from me."

"Let me help you," Gavin said.

Using the wall of the building, she used it as leverage to help her up. Once standing, she wobbled, her head felt dizzy.

Seeing she was about to pass out, Gavin grabbed her.

"I said don't touch me," she said without resisting this time.

Gavin felt the warm wet spot on her side. He looked at his hand and saw it was covered in blood. "You're hurt…bad."

"I see you're observant," Abigail snapped, finding some strength to again stand on her on.

Gavin looked closer at her face and suddenly realized he recognized her face. "Wait, you're that woman from the gunfight the other night."

She pushed him out of the way and walked a few steps before pausing to rest against the side of the building.

"Are you in some sort of trouble?" he asked.

Abigail's breathing had increased, and sweat was streaming down her face. The pain in her side was searing. Sensing he was a nice person, due mainly to his polite manners, Abigail decided to see if he could help her. "I need to get bandaged up. Can you help?"

"Sure, I can take you to the hospital. I think it's just down the street," he said, pointing the way she'd just come from.

"I can't go there," she said.

"But you're hurt real bad. Have you been shot?" he asked.

"Yeah, but the bullet went clean through. I just need a safe place to rest," she said.

"I'll take you back to wherever you were staying, tell

me," he said, still seemingly oblivious to her predicament.

"I can't go there. I can't go to the hospital. I have some men trying to kill me; they killed my partner, I need…to…find," Abigail said. Her legs buckled and she began to fall to the ground.

Gavin caught her and cradled her limp body in his arms. He looked around at a few passersby, but no one took an interest. They only assumed they were two drunks. "Oh no," he said, feeling awkward with a woman in his arms. He'd never held a woman before, especially like this. If she couldn't go to the hospital, then where could he take her? Not back to his quarters; that would most certainly put him in a tough spot with Elmer. An idea then popped into his head. He lifted her off the ground and held her close to his body and started for Saint John's Church.

***

Gavin first tried the church but found it empty. He then remembered that Aidan and Finnegan lived on the property in something called a rectory. He walked around until he found a small house behind the church. He banged on the door repeatedly until he saw a light come on in the window.

The door opened, and there was Finnegan standing there, holding a candle, rubbing his eyes. "Gavin?"

"Father, I need your help," he said.

Finnegan's eyes widened in shock, not at the sight of Gavin at his door, but of him holding a woman who looked injured. "Come on in, please. Put her on the couch there."

Aidan called from down the hall "Finn, who's that?"

"It's Gavin and a…friend," Finnegan answered. He placed the candle on a side table and lit an oil lamp for more light. Soon the room was aglow.

Gavin tenderly placed Abigail on the couch, propping her head up. "She's been shot…I think."

"Shot?" Finnegan asked, surprised to hear those words. He rushed to Abigail's side and lifted her bloody shirt to reveal the bullet hole. "You're right," he said. He reached his hand around to her back and found the exit wound. "It's passed through, thank the Lord."

"Can you help her?" Gavin asked.

"Why haven't you taken her to the local hospital? They have one here," Finnegan asked as he examined her for more wounds.

"She told me she couldn't go there. I think she's in a bit of trouble, Father," Gavin said, brushing the hair out of his face. He then noticed his hand was still bloody. Glancing down, he then saw his clothes were covered in her blood. He grunted, as these were his only nice clothes.

"Getting shot is usually an indicator of being in trouble. Hurry to the kitchen, fire up the oven, and place a pot of water on it," Finnegan ordered.

Gavin rushed off.

Aidan appeared from the hallway candle in his hand. He stepped into the front room and looked over Finnegan's back. "How badly hurt is the lad…wait, he is a she," Aidan said, finally noticing Abigail wasn't a man.

"Gavin said she's in trouble," Finnegan said just as he finished his examination. "No other wounds if you don't count cuts and bruises."

"I'd say getting shot is a sign you're in trouble," Aidan joked, repeating the same line Finnegan just said.

Gavin appeared with some clean towels and a bottle of whiskey. "Water is on and I found these. My mother had me get these items when my father cut his leg real bad a few years back."

Aidan and Finnegan looked at each other and smiled.

"You know a bit about caring for the wounded, I see." Aidan smiled.

"Help me get her clothes off," Finnegan ordered.

With the help of the other two, they quickly removed her bloody filthy clothes and neatly stacked them on the table.

Finnegan wiped down the excess blood around the wound until Gavin came with hot water; then he cleaned the wounds themselves. "Rip this into long strips," he ordered Gavin.

Gavin took a thin sheet and did as he said.

With the wounds on her front and back side clean and sanitized with the whiskey, he placed a thick clean towel over the wounds and used the strips to tie it to her side and back, then had her dressed in a spare set of his clothes.

Finished, he stood up and smiled. "I think she'll be fine. We'll need to watch for infection, but now we must let her rest."

"Gavin, join us in the kitchen," Aidan said, motioning for him to come.

Sitting around the table, Finnegan was the first to speak. "We said to come visit us on Sunday. We didn't mean bring a wounded young lass with you."

The joke brought levity to the situation and made everyone laugh.

"The night of the gunfight—"

"What gunfight?" Aidan asked. Neither he nor Finnegan had heard about the incident.

"Outside a house the other night there was a gunfight. The sheriff was killed. I heard the sounds, so I came down and saw her, that same woman, carrying a young girl away."

"You've seen her before tonight?" Aidan asked.

"Yes, Father, I saw her. I recognized her from the other night, but I didn't see the young girl with her. The next day I spoke to my employer, and he said she was a bounty hunter and along with some Pinkerton detectives had murdered the sheriff and others in a house."

"Hmm, that's an interesting story," Finnegan said, rubbing his chin.

"You said she was carrying a young girl?" Aidan asked.

"Yes, Father, and I saw other young girls and two other men. I suppose they were the Pinkerton detectives," Gavin replied before gulping down a glass of water.

"Do you suppose it's true, Father Leary?" Aidan asked.

"It might be," Finnegan said.

"What's true?" Gavin asked.

Aidan sighed loudly and clasped his hands together as if he were about to pray. "Son, before we came from Little Rock, we heard stories that there was a group abducting young children in these parts. Mainly girls but also boys, these poor souls were pressed into servitude."

"Slaves?" Gavin asked, shocked to hear such a thing could occur.

"Yes, slaves, but of a carnal nature. It's a disgusting and vile thing. The priest here before us had attempted to investigate the rumors and one day disappeared. Fortunately for us, he kept a diary and sent letters to the diocese. The thing is he went missing after he went to the sheriff with information that he had possibly discovered the main ringleaders behind this slave trade."

"You think they killed the priest?" Gavin asked. His jaw hung open.

"We do. We know Rome was informed of the matter but told the priest and others who had sounded the alarm to just allow the local authorities to handle it. What we fear is the local authorities are part of this evil cabal," Aidan replied.

"So you think she's one of the good ones? Do you think she might have rescued some of those children?" Gavin asked.

"Possibly, but until we know for sure, let's keep an eye on her and, most importantly, it's important we don't say a word about this to anyone," Aidan said.

"Yes, be as quiet as a church mouse," Finnegan joked.

"I won't utter a word, I promise," Gavin said.

"Now best you be off. We'll watch over her. Please do come back for eleven o'clock mass and lunch; then we'll give you an update on her condition," Aidan said, standing up and heading towards the front door.

"Thank you for allowing me to bring her here," Gavin said.

"Oh boy, look at your clothes. Do you have another set to wear?" Finnegan said.

"Just my work clothes, I plan on going back and washing them," Gavin said.

"Use cold water, it's the best for getting blood out," Aidan said.

"His clothes won't be ready by mass tomorrow," Finnegan said, rushing off. Moments later he returned with a stack of clothes. "These belonged to the other priest. I don't think he'll be needing them." He held up the trousers and said, "Looks like you two might have been the same size. Now run along. All of us need to rest."

Gavin took the clothes and rushed out of the house. He was again ever so thankful for having Aidan and Finnegan as friends and mentors of a sort. Without them, his life would most certainly be more difficult.

ELSTON, MISSOURI

Two wagons pulled up in front of a large plantation house.

In one wagon, Anna and Emma. In the other, the

other children who had been rescued the other night.

Like before, Anna and Emma found themselves kidnapped and their heads covered with sacks.

Emma was inconsolable from the second she was taken, while Anna reverted towards her stonier persona, her mind thinking of how she'd escape again.

The wagon stopped. Voices could be heard discussing what to do with them.

"Emma, I need you to be strong," Anna said.

"I can't, I can't do it. You don't know what it's like, Anna, you don't know," she cried.

Emma was right, Anna didn't know the pain and suffering Emma had felt, as she had seen the complete dark side of this journey while she hadn't. Regardless, Anna refused to give in, no matter what. "Emma, like before, I'll get us out of this, I will."

"Please do, please…I don't want them to hurt me, not like that," Emma cried.

A man laughed and said, "Oh, stop sniveling." He grabbed Emma and dragged her off the wagon. She lost her footing and toppled to the ground with a thud.

"Damn it, man, these are not sacks of beans, these are Baron's prized possessions. If you hurt them, I'll have you whipped," a man hollered.

"Sorry, Devon," the man said.

"Take her to the red room and take the other to the blue room. Don't hurt them; don't touch them. If I catch or hear that you, any of you, have touched them, you'll be shot. I'll repeat it one more time, these girls are our prized catch and are being held for our special guest at Monday night's party," Devon said.

Anna trembled when she heard how blunt the man Devon was being. A pair of hands took hold of her arm and pulled her towards the rear of the wagon. He then swooped her up and picked her up off the wagon and set her on the ground.

"Take them away. I'll have the maids come up and bathe them later," Devon barked.

Anna reached out and found Emma's hand. She clasped it tight and said, "It's me. Hold my hand tight; we're in this together, sister."

"I love you, Anna," Emma said.

"I love you too," Anna replied.

Escorted by a group of men, the girls disappeared into a darkened hallway of the house.

CHAPTER SIX

JEFFERSON CITY, MISSOURI

APRIL 12, 1891

Abigail heard the voices first but thought it was a dream. When she opened her eyes and looked around the small front room of the rectory, she then realized she wasn't in a dream at all. She abruptly sat up but recoiled from a sharp pain that shot through her body like a jolt of electricity. She looked down at her side and saw she was wearing someone else's clothing. She lifted up the shirt and looked at the bandage. She rubbed her hands along it, appreciating how well it had been applied, as if done with care.

"You're awake. How are you feeling?" Finnegan asked, holding a cup of tea in his hand and a big smile on his pudgy face.

"Who are you?" Abigail asked, her eyes darting around the room for her pistol. On the wall she saw a spear and a tomahawk hung as decorations.

"If you're looking for your firearm, you won't find it readily available. We have it stored in a safe place," Finnegan said. "And I see you staring at my tomahawk. I received that and the spear as a gift from a Cherokee chief after I completed a six-month mission with their tribe. A good man, never could get him to come over to Christ."

She swung her legs off the couch but stopped short of placing her feet on the floor due to the overwhelming pain.

"You need to rest. I can assure you that you're safe here," Finnegan said.

Aidan appeared from the kitchen. "How's our guest feeling?"

Abigail shot him a look and asked, "You helped me?"

"Of course, it's our duty in life to help others," Aidan said.

"Why?" she asked.

The two looked at each other, as they usually did, and smiled. "Like I said, it's our duty in life to help those in need."

"Where am I?" Abigail asked.

"You're in the rectory of Saint John's Church," Finnegan replied.

Finnegan took a few steps towards her.

Abigail scooted away, fearful he might hurt her.

Seeing her anxiety, he said, "If we meant you harm, we wouldn't have bandaged you up and given you safe haven. I merely want to look at the wound."

She thought for a quick second and came to the conclusion that he was speaking the truth. She lifted her shirt and turned her left side towards him.

Finnegan knelt down and lifted the bandage. "Looks good. You're lucky, very lucky. The Lord was looking after you last night."

"Getting shot isn't luck," she said.

"True, but if you end up being shot, it's luck that brings you a good man like Gavin and a place like this for you to rest and recuperate."

"Who's Gavin?" she asked.

"He's the young man who brought you here last night," Finnegan replied.

Abigail pressed her eyes closed and sorted through her memories until she came to Gavin's face and the encounter on the street. "I remember now."

"He carried you here after you told him you couldn't go to the hospital, and I'm glad he did," Aidan said.

"Thank you," Abigail said.

"Maybe thanks should be offered to you as well," Finnegan said, lowering her shirt and taking a seat in a chair opposite the couch.

"Thanks to me?" Abigail asked, sitting back on the couch and easing the pain in her side.

"You're here to save the children, aren't you?" Aidan asked.

Surprised by the question, she asked, "What do you know about it?"

Aidan also sat down and said, "We know quite a bit, and we'd like to help you."

***

Harrison again returned to Abigail's hotel room to find it as he'd left it hours before. "Where the hell is she?" he asked.

A man stepped in behind him and said, "Baron

wishes to see you."

"Go back and tell him I'm still looking for the girl. I don't have time to have meetings," Harrison growled.

"He insists," the man said.

Harrison spun around and pointed a finger at the man. "I'm not like you. I don't work for him in that capacity. He hired me to do a job, and until I'm finished with that job, I don't need to go waste my time talking to him. The next time I see him, we'll be discussing how he'll pay me for the job completed."

The man gulped and said, "I'll tell him."

"Now run off unless you have something else to tell me."

"We've placed the body up for display in front of Nick's Saloon," the man said, referring to Dwight's body. Harrison knew Abigail was famously loyal, and the second she heard his body was being displayed as a criminal in front of a saloon for all to see and ridicule, she'd come out of hiding.

"Good, and what about the man from the newspaper?" Harrison asked.

"We have him too. That's why Baron wishes to see you. He has a use for him."

Harrison thought and said, "Why didn't you say that to begin with?"

"I didn't think it mattered. No one ever says no to Baron," the man answered.

"I'll come see Baron; then I'm heading back out to find that bounty hunter," Harrison said.

ELSTON, MISSOURI

Harrison had only met Baron once, and that was in the back room of a bar on the day he arrived in Jefferson City; now he'd go to his estate in the country. He didn't think much of the man; he found him to be an undisciplined slob on account he was very fat. Judging people based upon appearances was a flaw of his, which had failed him before, most recently with Abigail. He never imagined a young, small woman could handle herself so well in a fight, yet here he was, a seasoned lawman turned mercenary, unable to capture or kill her.

He suspected Baron wished to discuss many things, one of which being why he hadn't been able to get Abigail yet, but he would assure him it was a matter of when not if.

The plan from before he'd even arrived was to prevent Milton and the bounty hunters from gathering information or finding out who was behind the child-abduction ring; but once that failed, he was left with the final plan: kill everyone. So far the fail-safe plan had worked; the only thing standing in his way was Abigail.

The carriage took him through a large bronze gate. Ahead, a long straight drive spanned a quarter mile lined with large oak trees. From the looks of it, Baron lived on an old plantation. At the end of the drive, a circular drive wrapped around. Large, wide stone steps met the drive and led guests into a massive set of double doors adorned with brass knockers and knobs.

The carriage stopped and the door opened.

Harrison looked up to the doors before exiting. When he did, several men stepped up to him. They were armed, and by the looks of it, they were guards.

A well-groomed man wearing a cropped suit jacket and pleated trousers emerged from the double doors and sauntered down the stairs. His long hair was slicked and pulled back tight into a ponytail that dangled down, touching his shoulders. He was Baron's right-hand man and confidant and went by the name Devon. "Mr. Harrison, Baron is looking forward to seeing you and getting an update."

Harrison grimaced at the man and asked, "Let's get this over with. I have a job to get back to."

"This way," Devon said then started back up the stairs.

Inside the house, Harrison gazed upon the ornate marble slab floor and columns that outlined the large foyer. A wide staircase, spanning twenty feet, stood in the center of the room. At the top of it stood Baron, his left hand tucked in his vest and his right hand holding a gold-topped walking stick. "Mr. Harrison, so good to see you." He slowly came down the stairway, taking each step with diligent care until he reached the bottom. He walked over to Harrison and held out his hand.

Harrison took it and said, "Baron."

"Come, let us go to the study and discuss all these troubles," Baron said and sauntered off down a long wide hallway, on the walls of which hung various portraits of Baron himself in different poses.

Harrison looked at each portrait with disdain, his

displeasure growing with each passing portrait.

Inside the expansive study, Baron went to his desk and sat down. He crossed his legs, unlike a man normally would, and relaxed into the thick cushioned chair.

Harrison sat down across the desk from him in a much smaller chair, his hat in his lap.

"We've got quite a mess now, don't we?" Baron said.

"Sometimes jobs have obstacles," Harrison said.

"I paid good money to my friend in Chicago to have you come when I heard Pinkertons were being sent. You were supposed to ensure this investigation went nowhere, but I keep hearing from my little spies in town that it's not, and now the sheriff is dead, killed by those bounty hunters, and the governor has taken notice too. He's not happy."

"Like I said, sometimes there are obstacles. It will get worked out," Harrison said bluntly. "I spoke to the governor; I assured him this will be taken care of."

"Tell me, Mr. Harrison, how goes the search for this female bounty hunter?" Baron asked.

"I'll have her soon. I know she's wounded, as we found a blood trail in the hospital that led out the back. We lost the trail later on, but I'm confident I'll have her very, very soon."

"Good, I don't need loose lips running around talking, I especially don't need any more attention than I already have. This business with the sheriff has definitely brought that and has cost me a lot of money that I don't wish to spend."

"Your man said you have Mr. Fisk and that you have

a plan," Harrison said.

"Yes, you see, Mr. Fisk is an accomplished writer for a paper in Kansas City. His articles are even picked up by others and reprinted. You see, he has reach and we could use that to our advantage," Baron said.

"How so?" Harrison asked as his eyes caught the sight of a bird landing on the windowsill behind Baron.

"We will get him to write an extensive news article on how these bounty hunters were involved in kidnapping children and selling them. You see, Mr. Harrison, we won't run from the story; it's probably out there. We will shape it to fit our needs, a deflection of sorts. Cast the blame on someone else."

Harrison shook his head. "It won't work."

"And why is that?" Baron asked.

"On account that you can't with confidence know he won't retract the story later," Harrison said.

"My dear Mr. Harrison, are you assuming he will be around later to retract?"

Knowing now what he intended, Harrison nodded. "I understand, but are you sure he'll write this article?"

"He's not willing to oblige us now, but I have a couple of men that are good at convincing people to do what I want," Baron said with a devilish smile.

Harrison knew that meant Fisk was being tortured. He also knew that eventually every man breaks. Suddenly, a concern popped in his head. "I still think it's a bad idea."

"Tell me what vexes you," Baron said, folding his delicate hands.

Harrison stared at a bead of sweat coursing down Baron's thick chubby face. His pale pasty skin and large swollen body made him look like a tick that had been attached to a dog for weeks, sucking every ounce of blood it could get. The reality was that Baron was a sort of bloodsucker; he bled his victims of their soul by abuse. He was absolutely repulsed by the man and by his business, but the money he was getting paid would ensure he'd never have to work again.

"You're awful quiet," Baron said.

Snapping out of his inner thoughts, Harrison said, "If you're not wanting attention, then you shouldn't have him write an article at all. It will draw people here, some of whom I used to work with. Thing is, there are some honorable US Marshals still out there that would flood in here to investigate."

Baron laid his head back against the chair and thought. "You know, you're right. I was looking at this as a way to deflect, but it would only highlight that there's something happening here. At the moment no one outside town is privy to what's happening."

"I strongly suggest that you clean up all loose ends and do it as fast as you can," Harrison said.

"I agree," Baron said, snapping his fingers at Devon, who stood lingering in the corner like a voyeur.

Devon rushed out of the room.

"I say, that business you did with the Fultons was…brutal, that's the best way to put it," Baron said, smiling.

"They were loose ends," Harrison said, referring to

disposing of Edward and Clara Fulton.

"I'd ask what you did, but that would be information I don't need to know," Baron said.

Outside the window behind Baron, Harrison spotted two men dragging Fisk to a brick wall and standing him against it. He leaned in to get a better look over Baron's shoulder.

Devon took a pistol from a guard, walked up to Fisk, pointed the gun at him, and pulled the trigger.

Fisk toppled to the ground dead.

Baron had used the word *brutal* to describe him, but it best fit Baron.

Baron looked over his shoulder and said, "Loose ends." He turned back to Harrison and said, "Mr. Harrison, thank you for this conversation and your insight. I'm having a party tomorrow night and would normally invite you, but I think you have some loose ends of your own to tidy up."

***

Harrison was plagued with a stream of thoughts and ideas as well as concerns about the situation he'd gotten himself involved with. It was an unsavory business, but he kept putting that out of his mind and thought only of collecting his money and retiring far away.

Devon escorted him back to the carriage and carried on a one-sided conversation. Talking about Fisk, the weather and even the price of tobacco, a crop that Baron grew on his vast expanses of land.

Harrison stopped him on the steps and asked, "Baron, is that his name, or was it a title at one time?"

"No, it's a name, a family name. He's the fourth, actually," Devon answered.

"And all this land, where did he get it from?" Harrison asked, looking out across the fields.

"He inherited it from his father, who passed away years ago."

"So Baron hasn't had to work a day in his life. That's what you're telling me?" Harrison asked.

"He's been fortunate, but I don't think it's fair to say he hasn't worked. One may inherit wealth, but it takes an intelligent and savvy individual to continue to grow that. Baron has done that."

"And this other business…why?"

"Why not?" Devon answered with a question. "Baron sees a need and fills it. There has been since the dawn of time a desire for the things we sell. Otherwise he wouldn't deal in it. I'm proud to say that Baron's planning on expanding out of this area and into other cities."

"But he finds these children in other states and brings them here?" Harrison asked.

Devon cocked his head and asked, "Why all the questions, Mr. Harrison?"

"Curious is all. Let's just say I'm fascinated in how people make money. Soon I'll have a considerable amount and was wondering what I should do with it."

"I hope you're not thinking of going into business as a competitor against Baron," Devon said.

"That will never happen. What you're doing is

disgusting, it makes my stomach turn, but it's a payday for me. I had some debts, and now they'll be paid off, and I'll have enough left so I can just ride off into the sunset and never see you, Baron or this shit state again."

"I wish you the best of luck, Mr. Harrison, I really do, and please get the job done as quick as you can. Baron is a patient man to a point," Devon said. "And, Mr. Harrison, can I assume you won't be attending the party tomorrow night?"

Several men grunted in the distance as they hauled off Fisk's body.

Harrison ignored his last question, got into the carriage, and slammed the door.

"Have a good day, Mr. Harrison," Devon said, waving obnoxiously.

Harrison grunted. He removed a flask from his jacket and took a swig. The sooner he could be done with this business, the better.

***

Anna was free to walk around the room she was being held in. Of course she tried the door but found it locked, and the single window that overlooked the side of the property was boarded up, only slits allowing the sun to come through.

Every hour on the hour, like clockwork, someone would enter the room to check on her. Sometimes they brought her food with no utensils and water in a pail, or left her with a pail to use as a toilet.

A lone candle lit the space, giving her enough light to see. She was tempted to use it to set the room on fire, but that had its risks. Getting burned alive wasn't something she wanted to have happen. Like on the train, she needed something, a weapon to fashion out of anything. There weren't any mirrors to break, nor could she find anything to break off to use. Feeling hopeless, she sat on the bed, pondering what would happen. *Why is this my life? How could God allow this to be?* So many questions tortured her mind.

Frustrated, she got up and again started pacing. She needed to get out of there and go find her sister. *But where is the red room?*

Her body still wasn't one hundred percent. The wound in her shoulder wasn't healed nor was the gunshot. She was a mess but yet determined.

Over and over she recited to herself, *There has to be a way out of here. There has to be a way out of here. There has to be a way out of here.* She knew giving in meant whatever horrible thing was going to happen for sure, but if she tried to resist, tried to fight back, only then would she have a chance to prevent it. She didn't have any other options. She prayed Abigail would come for her or that those Pinkertons might find them; but like before, she couldn't let fate decide. Relying on fate was for fools, her father used to tell her, and it was true. Fortune came to those who tried, and try she would.

JEFFERSON CITY, MISSOURI

Upon hearing the news about Edward and Clara Fulton, Abigail lost her appetite. She pushed her plate aside and stared down at the table, distraught.

"A parishioner, a chatty one, told me they found their bodies along the shore of the river early this morning," Aidan said sadly. "I hear the governor is even looking into the matter now."

"You said you were working for Mr. Fulton?" Aidan asked.

"Yes, he employed me to find his daughters," Abigail replied. "Have you heard anything about my friend Mr. Fisk?"

"Nothing, I asked a few parishioners, but no one heard about him. All they kept talking about was the sheriff being murdered and now the Fultons. Having a man like Mr. Fulton murdered in town will most definitely bring some people looking, don't you think?" Finnegan asked.

Gavin sat at the far end of the table, speechless. He had found himself involved in something he wasn't sure he wanted to be associated with. He had been raised to help those in need but also raised to avoid situations that could affect him negatively.

"You two mentioned this other priest had a diary and that contained in its pages could be clues to who Baron is and where we might find him," Abigail said, shifting in her seat.

"Yes," Aiden said, reaching behind him and picking

up a black hardcover book. He placed it in front of him and opened it. He thumbed through the cream-colored pages until he reached the passage he was looking for. *"I have kept asking, and now I know who the individual in charge of this evil enterprise is. His name is Baron. I had thought that could have been a title, but it is not. That is his name. I came to have this information after a follower revealed it in confession. I know I am to keep what is expressed in confessions confidential, but something of this nature must be exposed. I plan on writing a letter to Rome and to the monsignor in Little Rock, asking their advice in this matter."*

"Is that it?" Abigail asked.

"No, there is more," Aidan said, flipping to another page. He smoothed out the book with his hand and read, *"The same follower came into confession again. He claimed to have been witness to horrible acts at the estate owned by Baron. He talked about how excited he was to visit the old plantation for a party until he saw the most horrible things being done to young children. I asked him to give more details, but this prompted him to flee the confessional. I hope to see him soon. I heard from Rome, and they told me not to concern myself with such matters and to inform the local authorities. I plan on doing so tomorrow."*

"Baron lives on an old plantation. How many old plantations can there be around here?" Abigail asked, thinking there couldn't be that many.

"We will find out," Finnegan said.

"Yes, we'll ask around, tell people we're interested for historical reasons," Aidan said.

"Just don't attract too much attention," Abigail said.

"We won't. We're good that way," Finnegan said, smiling.

Abigail fidgeted with her plate, looked up from the table, and asked, "Why are you helping me? And don't give me the same line you did earlier."

"Because we can't sit back and allow evil to destroy lives. We both joined the church to make a difference and to spread the word of God. That also means taking a stand," Aidan replied.

"But, Father, you told me the last priest was most likely killed," Gavin said, finally speaking up.

"He most likely did. And if he did get killed, he died a martyr, fighting to protect the innocent," Aidan replied.

"So you'll help me?" Abigail asked.

"Yes, we will do what we can while remaining anonymous. This is not to protect us but to allow us to work in the open. We will be your eyes and ears," Aidan said.

"Nice way to put it," Finnegan said, patting Aiden on the arm.

"Thank you," Abigail said. "What I need to do now is go find Fisk."

"No, you need to heal. You can't be seen in public; you sort of stick out like a sore thumb," Finnegan said. "Let us look around, ask; you remain here, get healthy so you can fight the fight."

She hated to admit it, but he was right. The thought of sitting around made her feel useless, but if she went out now, the chances of her success were limited.

Finding the courage, Gavin asked, "What can I do?"

"Nothing, you've done enough. You need to go back to work tomorrow and forget you know anything about this," Aidan said.

"Agreed," Finnegan replied.

"I can't do that. If there are children in need, I want to help," Gavin declared.

"You're just a boy; let the adults handle this," Abigail said.

"I'm not a boy; I'm tired of people saying that. I'm eighteen and just small for my age. You for one should know that size doesn't define performance or ability," Gavin snapped at Abigail.

"You're right, I apologize," she said. "But they're also right. There isn't anything you can realistically do. The men who control this operation are cleaning up anything that will lead anyone to them. If they find out you're a part of this, they'll dispose of you like they did the Fultons."

"Let me help by providing support, then. I'll make runs for you, bring supplies. Please let me do something," Gavin said.

The three looked at each other.

"You can help me in the church after hours. This will free me up to go out in town and visit parishioners. They're our best resource for information right now," Aiden said.

"I can do that," Gavin said.

"And you must not under any circumstances disclose this to anyone else, not even your employers," Aidan said, knowing Gavin liked to talk.

"I won't say a thing, I already told you that," Gavin said.

Abigail lowered her head again. She could feel a heavy fatigue weighing on her.

"And you, my dear lassie, need to go rest, c'mon," Finnegan said, getting up and taking Abigail by the arm.

"I'm fine," she protested.

"No, you're not, and we're done here for now. We have what we need to do, and what you need to do is rest. Now come with me," Finnegan said.

Abigail relented. She stood with Finnegan's aid and let him lead her to the couch.

Aiden and Gavin said their goodbyes and left the house.

Alone with her, Finnegan wanted to know a bit more about the mysterious bounty hunter who was resting on his couch. "Tell me a bit about yourself," he said, tucking in a blanket around her.

"There's nothing to say," she answered, deliberately avoiding the question.

"I will not allow you to lie here, eat my food, and not share with me who you are. We all have stories to tell. Mine, I'm sure, is not as exciting as yours, but you must have parents, a home, maybe even children."

Abigail reacted slightly when he mentioned children.

"You do have children. I saw it in your eyes when I uttered the word," Finnegan said.

She was tired and normally wouldn't talk with anyone about the topic, but with Finnegan being a priest, she felt more at ease. "I wouldn't call her a daughter, as I didn't give birth to her, but I rescued a little girl a few years ago. Her name is Madeleine. She lives in Dallas with a nice family."

"But you care for her," Finnegan said.

"Who wouldn't? She's precious. I tried to go it alone, that is, be her parent and still do this job, but it was too much. I was gone all the time, and each job I'd get, she'd beg me not to go, but I had to. I don't know how else to make money, and I'm not about to get married so I can have security. After more than a few times leaving her, I decided it was best to have her live with the family that watched her. The last time I saw her, I told her I wasn't coming back…" Abigail said, pausing as tears welled in her eyes.

"That hurt her, didn't it?" Finnegan asked.

"It did."

"And you too," Finnegan said.

"It crushed me. I felt like I had just ripped my own heart out and stomped on it, but I knew over time that I'd feel better; the thing is, I don't. I was told that time heals all wounds, but this won't heal. It still hurts when I think about her, about as much as when it happened," she confessed.

"Love is an amazing thing. It is one of God's greatest gifts to us," he said.

"It feels like a curse now. I don't think about her when I'm working, but the second I sit still for any length of time, she comes to my thoughts and the pain follows," Abigail said, wiping a tear away from her cheek. "I'm sorry, I'm acting like a child."

"You're not acting like a child, you're acting like a human being, one of God's children who deeply loves another and is missing them."

"I need to purge her from my mind. When I feel this way, I feel weak," she said.

Finnegan took her hand and gently caressed it. "My dear, you're not weak; you must be the toughest woman next to the Blessed Mother Mary that I've ever met. What you're willing to do and sacrifice for these lost children makes you a very special and strong woman."

"If no one else stands up to defend them, who will?" she asked.

"The weaker ones in our society need people like you. Evil exists in this world and must be confronted."

"I agree, Father," she said.

"Are you a religious person, Abigail?" he asked.

"No, and I don't think I'll ever be, but I do believe in something bigger than myself. I don't know what it is, but it exists," she answered.

"That's God, my dear," he said.

"How can I move on from Madeleine, Father?" she asked, genuinely wanting to have someone tell her what to do. It was something she hadn't done in a long time.

"Why do you have to move on? Forgive me for my bluntness, but you must not move on from the child, you must embrace her. What I'm saying is that child needed you, and I don't believe she's done needing you. Maybe you can't be her mother, but you can be a teacher, a mentor, a friend…and I daresay family to her. She needs you in whatever capacity you can give yourself. Don't abandon her. Be with her when you can; give her the gift of your time when it's appropriate so that you can teach her what you've learned. You have a tremendous amount to share."

"That sounds like what my partner told me but not as eloquent."

"It's mainly the accent. We sound smarter because we have it, that's all," he joked.

The two laughed.

"When we're done here, I suggest the first thing you do is go to her. Maybe send her a telegram so she knows you're coming and it's not a surprise. This will give her time to prepare for your arrival," Finnegan advised.

"I think I'll do that," she said.

"Good, now I'll leave you be. Call out if you need anything," Finnegan said, got up, and left the room.

Abigail's heart filled with hope suddenly. In the span of days, her most trusted partner and a man of God had given similar advice on how to handle the situation with Madeleine. She'd heed their advice and go see Madeleine when she was done in Jefferson City; then reality hit her. First she'd have to survive her current situation in order for that to happen.

CHAPTER SEVEN

JEFFERSON CITY, MISSOURI

APRIL 13, 1891

Gavin fought the urge to tell Elmer everything. He so wanted to share what he'd seen and done over the remaining part of the weekend.

Elmer emerged from the front office and called out, "Gavin, come here, and hurry up."

Gavin put the broom aside and ran up to him. "Yes, sir."

"There's a case of proof books in a box on the loading dock. I need you to deliver it here," Elmer said, giving him an address and directions on how to get there.

"Yes, sir," Gavin said happily. He was excited to finally get out and see some of the town and possibly the countryside.

"Make sure when you deliver it, you get them to sign the bill of lading. We'll need it for our records," Elmer said.

"I'll do that," Gavin said.

"Now away with you, and hurry back. I have a shipment of paper coming in later; I'll need you down at the riverfront to fetch it for us," Elmer said.

"I'll be back in time, don't you worry," Gavin said, running towards the back. He loaded the box into the wagon, climbed on and hurried away.

ELSTON, MISSOURI

Gavin followed the directions to the letter and arrived at a large estate. He stared at the massive house in awe at the splendor. He wondered if someone of royalty lived there.

A man exited the house and asked, "May I help you?"

Gavin looked at the paper and said, "I'm making a delivery for Clancy Printing House. I have a box of book proofs for a Devon."

"I can take them," the man said.

"I'm to deliver them to him, it says here, and I need a signature," Gavin said.

The man gave Gavin a look of annoyance and briskly walked back inside the house.

Moments later Devon appeared at the top of the stairs. He rushed down and said, "Are these the proofs? Oh my, he's been waiting for them. I need to see." He pulled a single hardback book from the box and opened it. "I love the smell of the printed page."

"They are nice-looking books," Gavin said, smiling.

Devon turned the crisp pages, his eyes scanning the words.

"Sir, if you're Devon, do you mind signing this? That way I can be on my way," Gavin said, handing him the bill of lading.

Devon tore his gaze from the book, looked at the paper he was being handed, then to Gavin. "Aren't you a handsome boy?"

Feeling awkward, Gavin said, "Here's a pencil to

sign."

The door at the top of the stairs opened and out stepped Baron. He rubbed his belly and cried out, "I say, Devon, are those the proofs?"

"Yes, they are. Baron, you must come see," Devon replied.

The second Gavin heard the name, his body tensed and his stomach churned to the point he wanted to vomit. He looked around the property. It was immense, endless fields rolled, all filled with newly planted crops, and at the center of it all was a huge home. He came to realize he was on a plantation estate, but this wasn't any plantation, this was the one owned by Baron, the man Abigail was looking for.

Baron barreled down the stairs, snatched the book from Devon's hand, and examined it closely. "Nice, okay, um, don't like that, yes, like that, looks good; it's beautiful, don't you say? I can't wait to show these at the party later."

"I think it's beautiful too. Baron, you can count yourself an author now," Devon said.

"Who's this?" Baron asked, looking up and seeing Gavin.

"He's the delivery boy from Clancy's," Devon answered.

"Sir, if you could please sign so I can be on my way," Gavin said nervously, not making eye contact with either of them.

"Why don't you come inside for a drink? You must be thirsty, and it's a long ride back into town," Baron suggested.

"No, sir, I can't. I must be getting back. My employer is expecting me soon; I have other work to get done," Gavin replied.

Devon cooed, "Oh, come, boy, we don't bite."

Holding back the urge to vomit, Gavin grew agitated. "Sir, I need to be going."

"Isn't he a grumpy thing." Baron laughed.

Devon grabbed the books and snapped, "Off with you, then."

Wanting nothing but knowing he needed that signed bill of lading, Gavin again asked, "Can you please sign it and give it back to me?"

"Let me do it," Baron said, taking the paper and pencil and signing his name in big bold letters so that it easily could be read. He walked over so he was standing next to Gavin and shoved the paper deep into his pocket. "Make sure your employer knows that when the finished books are done, I wish for you to deliver them."

"Thank you, sir, have a good day," Gavin said, slapping the reins of the horse hard. The wagon lunged forward. Gavin repeatedly whipped the horse so it would go faster. Behind him he heard the two laughing about their encounter with him.

***

Back in the house, Baron said to Devon, "I want to see our little princesses, make sure they're ready for tonight."

"Of course, I personally have been checking, and

they're cleaned up and presentable. The governor will be thrilled. As you know, he's very grateful you fetched them. Ever since he first set eyes on them months ago in Topeka with Edward Fulton, he's desired them. He was very disappointed by what happened the other night, but now that you have them back, he's excited to see them," Devon said.

"The governor has been one of my best clients," Baron said, finally exposing how deep the conspiracy went. "He pays well and on time. He's unlike some of the other politicians, especially that senator from Iowa; he's a stingy one."

"Come, let's go see the girls," Devon said.

Upstairs, Baron visited Emma first. He examined her as if she were a piece of cattle he was going to sell on the market. He had her stand, turn and made her practice reciting lines. He threatened her if she didn't comply and told her that only good things would come if she obliged the governor upon his visit.

Terrified, Emma relented and pledged to do whatever he requested.

When Baron visited Anna, though, he found a girl who wasn't as compliant.

"I won't do what you say," Anna spat.

"Listen, you'll do as I, Devon or any of my clients say; if you don't, I'll hurt your sister. Do you hear me?" Baron growled.

"Go to hell," Anna barked.

Baron looked at Devon and chuckled. "She's got a fire in her. It appears she needs to be broken. I'll tell the governor that when he arrives."

"The governor?" Anna asked.

"Yes, my dear girl, the governor of this great state has had his eye on you and your lovely sister since he met you a while back when he visited your house in Topeka. I believe he and your father were working on a deal for a railway passage from Springfield to Kansas City. It was he who paid me to get you girls."

Anna began to hyperventilate when told who was ultimately behind it all.

"Just be calm and it will all be over soon. If you just give in, it will be much easier," Baron said, walking over to touch her hair.

Anna shrugged off his touch and barked, "I'm still hurt. I've been punctured and shot. You think he wants this?" she asked, pulling down the shoulder of her dress to expose the wound in her shoulder.

"You could be more presentable, but this will do," he said. He turned to Devon and said, "Come, let's go make sure the final preparations are done for the party."

The men left the room.

Anna's strength melted away. She dropped to the floor and nearly vomited. She cleared her negative thoughts, and with grit, she clenched her hands and got back to her feet. "I will find a way."

JEFFERSON CITY, MISSOURI

Taking a cue from Abigail and Dwight, Harrison went from saloon to saloon, asking if anyone had seen anything out of the ordinary or had seen Abigail since their gunfight the other night; to his chagrin, the answer he kept getting was no.

With only a few bars and saloons left to go, he made his way into the Lazy Susan Saloon. It was bristling with activity for a late afternoon. He pushed his way to an open spot at the bar and called out to the bartender.

Seeing Harrison, the bartender, a man by the name of Adam, made his way down. "What can I get ya?"

"I need information," Harrison said.

"What sort of information?" Adam asked.

"Have you seen a woman—wears trousers, carries a pistol—come in here since late the other night?"

"Nope, can't say I have," Adam said.

"You sure?" Harrison asked.

"I'm telling you, mister, I ain't seen any woman wearing trousers and carrying a pistol. If you're not drinking, I need to be getting back to work," Adam said.

"I'm done," Harrison said.

Adam huffed and moved away.

Crossing this establishment off the list, Harrison turned to leave.

"Hey, I saw a woman the other night just outside the place. She looked hurt, real bad," an old man said from the far end of the bar.

Harrison made his way over and asked, "When?"

"Saturday night, late, maybe around eleven or so," the old man said, taking a sip of whiskey.

"And she was wearing?"

"Yeah, just like you described her. She looked like a

cowboy, had all the attire on. I was headin' home after playing poker and almost ran into her and some young feller."

"Who?" Harrison asked with urgency in his voice.

The old man started to rub his brow as he thought. "Let me see here. I met the young feller too. He works for…"

"Who, damn it?" Harrison spat.

The old man gave Harrison a harsh look and spat back, "Don't get ornery with me, you son of a bitch. I'm tryin' to help you out."

Regretting his tone, Harrison said, "I apologize. It's just that I really need to find her."

"Is she a lady friend of yours?" the old man asked.

"We're acquaintances, and I heard she was hurt. I want to see if she's okay," Harrison lied.

"Hey, Adam, that young feller who was in here on Saturday night, the naïve one, his boss knows the owner of the Lazy Susan, what's his name?" the old man asked Adam.

Adam shook his head, annoyed he was still being asked questions.

"C'mon, Adam, help me out. Who's that feller?" the old man asked.

"Elmer Fitzpatrick from Clancy Printing House," Adam said.

The old man turned, but Harrison was already on his way out the door. "Hey, don't you want to know his name?"

"I got all I need," Harrison said as he exited out the

door.

***

Gavin arrived at the town limits but was torn on what to do. Should he go directly to see Abigail or go to the riverfront and get the crate of paper? He didn't want to be late picking up the crate, but the information he had was valuable. It was literally life or death for all those children.

Compelled to do what was righteous, he rode for the rectory. As he passed Nick's Saloon, he saw a body standing in a coffin propped up in front of Nick's Saloon. He slowed and saw a placard hung around the man's neck that read, *"You kill our sheriff, we kill you."*

Realizing who it was, he whipped the horse to ride hard and fast until he reached the rectory. He leapt off the wagon and ran to the front door and began to bang. "Abigail, Father Harris!"

Finnegan opened the door. "Son, what's wrong?"

Gavin raced inside panting heavily. Back and forth he paced the room, mumbling gibberish. "They have his body, yeah, his body, and Baron, I know where he is, yeah."

"Gavin, you're crazed. Sit down and relax," Finnegan said, trying to stop Gavin from pacing the room.

"I saw him, yeah, I did, but, Abigail, I also saw his body!" Gavin railed.

Abigail got up from the couch, walked over to him, and slapped his face. "Calm down!"

Her slap did the trick. Gavin stopped his erratic behavior. He looked at her and said, "Your partner, his body, they have it in front of Nick's Saloon with a sign on it that reads, 'You kill our sheriff, we kill you.'"

"What?" she barked.

"I saw it coming into town. They have it propped up like he's some sort of ornament for display," he cried.

Her temper flared. She ripped off the clothes she had on, paying no mind to who was in the room, and began to get dressed in her own clothes.

"Where are you going?" Finnegan asked.

"Do I need to say?" she replied, pulling her shirt over her head.

"You can't go out there. That's what they want. It's probably a ruse to draw you out," Finnegan said.

"I don't give a damn. If they want a fight, I'll fight them. I'll kill every last one of them," she barked, now sitting on the couch and slipping her boots on.

"Where's Aiden when I need someone with a calming voice?" Finnegan said.

"I-I also met Baron," Gavin finally confessed.

Abigail and Finnegan both stopped what they were doing, turned and faced him.

"Where?" Abigail asked.

"I had to deliver a crate of books out in the countryside. It was a plantation. I didn't think anything of it; I admit I wasn't really listening to everything until I heard his name. He's a disgusting person. He propositioned me, said something about a party tonight," Gavin said.

Abigail picked up her gun belt and swung it around her torso and cinched it. She could feel the pain in her side after doing it, but gritted her teeth and moved past it. She pulled the Colt, half-cocked it, and spun the cylinder.

"You can't go alone," Finnegan said, walking up to Abigail. "You're still hurt. You're going in there all alone, and he must have many men."

"I have her," she said, holding up her Colt and lowering the hammer before holstering it.

"That's all you're taking?" Finnegan asked.

"That's all I have," she said. "Never stopped me before."

Finnegan raced out of the room and returned quickly with an Ithaca double-barreled shotgun and a pouch of additional shells. "Take this with you. If you're not going to listen to reason, then go prepared."

"I thought you'd tell me to go with God," Abigail said.

"He's riding with you, I know that already," Finnegan said and embraced her.

Abigail turned to Gavin and asked, "Where is Baron?"

Gavin pulled the note from his pocket and handed it to her. "Follow these directions. It'll lead you there."

Abigail picked up her hat, put it on and smoothed out the brim. "Father, can I ask another favor of you?"

"Of course," Finnegan said.

"Can I borrow your horse?" she asked, heading towards the door.

"Yes, yes, anything," Finnegan replied.

Abigail's eyes passed over the tomahawk on the wall. She smiled and asked, "And can I take that too?"

***

Harrison checked his pistols before walking into the front office of the Clancy Printing House. He wasn't sure what to expect, and he wanted to ensure he was ready to go.

The front door opened, and out stepped Elmer's brother. He saw Harrison and asked, "Howdy, sir, can I help you with any printing today?"

Harrison didn't have time to chat and get the runaround, so he pulled his pistol, a Remington, cocked it and put it under his chin. "Back inside."

"Yessss, sir," he said, stuttering.

The two men walked inside and closed the door.

"Don't hurt me," Edwin said.

"I'm looking for the boy who works here. Where can I find him?"

"Gavin, you're looking for Gavin," Edwin said.

"Where's Gavin?" Harrison said.

"He's not here. He went on a delivery and a pickup, will be back soon."

"Anyone else here?" Harrison asked.

"Just me and my brother, Elmer; he's in the back on the printing floor."

"Call him in here. Don't warn him, or I'll put a hole in your head," Harrison warned, pushing the muzzle deeper into the flesh of his jowls.

"I-I won't, I swear it," Edwin said in a pleading tone.

"Call him," Harrison barked.

"Elmer, come up here!" Edwin cried out.

Seconds later the back door of the front office opened, and there stood Elmer, his hands and neck covered in black ink. "What do you need?"

Harrison pulled his second Remington, cocked it and pointed it at Elmer. "Get your ass in here and sit down in that chair," he said, motioning with his head towards a desk chair to his left. "And you sit in that chair."

Edwin did as he said, his body trembling from fear. "If it's money you need, we have it in the safe."

"I'm not here to rob you, I'm here to speak with Gavin," Harrison said.

"He's out for delivery; he should be arriving back any minute," Elmer said.

Harrison went to the front door and locked it. He closed the drapes and took another chair and sat down. "Where will he arrive, the back?"

"Yes," Elmer said.

"You, where can I find some rope?" Harrison asked.

"There's some in the back, on the right near the press," Elmer said.

Harrison stood and walked over to Elmer. "Get up." He turned to Edwin and said, "You too."

The men did as he said.

"Let's go into the back. We'll get you tied up and wait for Gavin to come back from deliveries."

Harrison led them into the back, tied them up, and sat near the door waiting.

ELSTON, MISSOURI

Anna heard a carriage ride up the gravel drive. She ran to the boarded window and peeked out to see the carriage arriving at the front. Several men ran up to it, with one opening the door.

Devon suddenly appeared and bowed when a man exited.

Anna looked closer and recognized the man; it was the governor. He was here, and that meant he'd be in her room very soon.

Breathing heavily, she tore herself away from the window and started to pace. "There has to be a way. There has to be a way."

She stared all around the room, looking for anything at all that she could use as a weapon. There had to be something, she thought, but a fear was growing that she wouldn't find something, that she wouldn't be able to escape this time. She'd been in the room for some time, yet she hadn't discovered anything to use.

Footsteps outside her door sent shivers down her spine.

Is this it?

The door unlocked and swung open. One of the maids who helped clean her up entered the room and went for the chamber pot.

Anna ran to her and grabbed her arm. "Please help me, please."

"Get your hands off me," the woman barked, pulling her arm back. She gave Anna a crazed look and said, "I suggest you accept your fate, girl."

"How can you let this happen?" Anna asked, shocked by her callous reply.

"I've been where you are. All I can say is you'll have to accept that this is now your life," she said.

"You were like me once?" Anna asked.

"Yes."

"Then help me. You know this isn't right," Anna pleaded.

The woman picked up the pot and headed for the door.

Anna spotted a hand mirror and brush in her apron pocket and got an idea. "Can I at least look presentable?"

Her question stopped the woman at the threshold. She turned and asked, "What do you want?"

"If I'm to accept my fate, can I at least look presentable?" Anna asked, nodding to the mirror and brush.

The woman glanced down and said, "I suppose." She pulled them out and handed them to Anna. "Hurry up."

Anna took the brush and began to run it through her hair while looking at her reflection in the mirror.

"Gwen, get down here!" a voice boomed down the hall.

The woman called out, "I'll be right there." She reached for the mirror and brush and said, "Time's up."

Anna stepped just out of her reach and said, "No, I need to make sure I look good."

"Gwen, get your ass down here now!" the voice boomed again.

Aggravated, Gwen snapped at Anna, "I'll be back for those." She stepped out of the room, slammed the door shut, and locked it.

Anna looked at her reflection in the mirror and smiled. She had her weapon; now she needed to get it ready so she could strike. She took it to the side table, set it at an angle against it, and stepped on it. The glass in the mirror snapped. With her slim fingers, she pried out a six-inch-long jagged piece and held it up to examine. It was perfect. Using a handkerchief, she wrapped half of it so she wouldn't cut her hand while gripping it. Now ready, she placed it in the palm of her hand and curled her fingers around it. Holding it over her head, she practiced how she'd use it against whomever she came into contact with.

Looking at it one more time in her small hand, she caressed the glass, smiled and said, "It's time to fight back."

***

Baron raced down the stairs. "Governor Strauss, so good to see you."

Strauss gave him an irritated scowl and said, "Baron, this entire thing has turned into a bloody mess. Can you promise me this will soon be cleared up?"

Baron rushed to Strauss, took his hand and said, "My dear Governor, I can assure you with absolute certainty that my man Harrison will have this all cleaned up soon. And I do have gratitude for allowing the use of some of your men to take care of the Fultons."

"Three of them are dead at the hands of that woman bounty hunter," Strauss growled.

"An unfortunate turn of events. She's quite good with a gun, it appears," Baron said, smiling.

"Do you find this to be funny?"

"Oh no, sir, not at all. As I've heard before, sometimes there are obstacles to deal with," Baron said, repeating a line from Harrison.

"Having the Fultons killed is not what I wanted to have happen. I'm now having it covered up as a robbery gone wrong. So many problems," Strauss said, walking towards the parlor, where he saw a couple of staff members with drink trays.

Baron followed by his side. "Can I assume you're here early to see your prize?"

"I am. I've waited long enough," Strauss said, taking a glass of champagne and putting it to his lips.

"Both are ready for you. I have them separated but can put them in the same room if that's what you wish," Baron said.

Strauss raised his brow as if in thought. "I like that idea; yes, put them together."

Baron turned to Devon, who, as usual, was hovering close by. "Go put the Fulton girls in the same room, and make sure they're ready. I believe our distinguished guest will be coming up soon."

Devon nodded and rushed off.

"Give us ten minutes."

"Very well," Strauss said, taking another drink.

"The one called Anna, she's been shot, as you know, but that hasn't stopped her from being a firecracker. You might have to tame her."

A devilish grin stretched across Strauss's face. "I'll enjoy that."

JEFFERSON CITY, MISSOURI

Gavin hurried to the dock to retrieve the crates of paper after Abigail had left. His concern that he would be late to pick them up was unfounded. He was able to retrieve the shipment and headed promptly back to the printing office.

His heart was thumping when he thought about what would happen to Abigail. He imagined all sorts of outcomes, from her getting killed to her saving the day and rescuing all the children. He did begin to wonder if his contribution would come back to haunt him. He had stepped up and showed courage, but deep down he was terrified. Maybe his father was right; just maybe he was still too young and naïve for the world. In a matter of days, he'd seen so much, more than most people, or was this normal? he then pondered. Was this life as an adult?

He parked the wagon, unloaded the heavy crates on the loading dock, and shoved them just inside the back door. Noticing it was dark on the printing floor, he went to light some lanterns. After getting the first lit, he caught the sight of something unusual in the corner of his eye. He turned and was met with the back of Harrison's hand. The blow to his face sent him reeling across an aisle and into a machine. He shook off the hit and turned to see where it had come from, only to get hit again. This blow drove him to his knees.

Then he heard the distinct click of a hammer on a pistol going back. He looked up and saw the black muzzle of a pistol pointed at him.

"Are you Gavin?" Harrison asked.

With his hands held high, Gavin answered, "Yes, sir."

"Good, get up," Harrison ordered.

"What do you want with me?" Gavin asked, getting to his feet.

Harrison grabbed him by the neck and shoved him forward until he reached the far wall. "Sit down next to your friends."

"Do what he says," Elmer pleaded.

"What's going on?" Gavin asked.

"I was hoping you'd know. He came here asking for you specifically," Edwin said.

Gavin gave Harrison a look to see if he recognized him but didn't. "What do you want, mister?"

"Sit down," Harrison ordered.

Gavin slid down the wall until he was sitting cross-legged on the floor.

Harrison leveled the pistol at Gavin's head and asked, "Where's Abigail?"

Hearing her name sent terror through his body.

"Are you deaf? Where's Abigail?" Harrison asked again.

Now Gavin knew what this was all about. The

concern he'd had earlier proved correct. This had come back to haunt him. He then heard his father's warnings booming in his head. *"The world is bad. The world is full of threats. You're too young, too naïve to go out into it."*

Tired of waiting for Gavin to reply, Harrison swung and smacked him with the back of his hand.

This hit split open Gavin's lip. He wiped the blood with his hand and looked at it. His heart was racing, beating so hard he could feel it throbbing in his head.

Harrison looked at Elmer and Edwin and asked, "Is he stupid?"

"Gavin, tell the man what he wants to know," Elmer begged.

Wiping the blood on his trousers, Gavin looked deep in Harrison's eyes and said, "I don't know who you're talking about."

"Don't lie to me, boy," Harrison growled.

Feeling a surge of courage, Gavin snapped, "I'm not a boy."

This comment prompted Harrison to laugh. "If you're a man, you're a damn small one."

Gavin's fear was turning to anger. The temptation to strike back was building up in him.

Harrison leaned in and pressed the muzzle against Gavin's forehead. "Tell me where Abigail is or die."

With steely eyes, Gavin slowly said, "I don't know who you're talking about."

Frustrated, Harrison pulled the pistol away and paced around the room. "Damn it, I don't want to kill you. I really don't." It was one of the most honest things

Harrison had ever said. He was willing to kill them, but deep down he didn't want to. He had grown tired of the bloodshed, but at the same time, the horse was out of the stable and galloping hard, as they say. He stepped back in front of Gavin and said, "I'm asking you one more time, and if you give me the same lie, I'll put a round through him right there."

Seeing Harrison pointing at him, Edwin whined, "Tell him what you know!"

If he told Harrison about Abigail, that would create a chain reaction that would ultimately lead back to Aidan and Finnegan. He couldn't allow that to happen. They had shown him generosity beyond anything he'd ever seen. They were good men, and if he betrayed Abigail, he'd be betraying them. No. He would have to risk Edwin's life and not give up Abigail. "I don't know who she is."

Harrison gritted his teeth. He shook his head and said, "I warned you." He pointed the pistol at Edwin and pulled the trigger, killing Edwin with a shot to the face.

"No, oh no, Edwin!" Elmer cried out. He struggled to free himself from the rope bindings but couldn't budge more than an inch.

With the knowledge that Harrison meant what he said and was capable of murder, it steeled Gavin even more. With Edwin dead, why not kill the rest of them? Did he really think giving up Abigail would save any of them now? No. In fact, giving away that knowledge would only get more killed. In his head, his father's voice was raging, telling him how weak or small or insignificant he was. He clenched his hands into fists and cast a deadly stare at Harrison.

"His blood is on your hands," Harrison said. "Now, are you going to tell me where Abigail is, or do I have to kill him next?"

Wailing in grief, Elmer lashed out at Gavin. "Tell him, damn you!"

"I'm sorry, Elmer, I'm so sorry," he said to Elmer then faced Harrison, "but I don't know who you're talking about."

"Then so be it," Harrison said as he placed his thumb on the hammer to cock it back.

Gavin sprang from his spot. He wrapped his arms around Harrison's waist, lifted him off his feet, turned and body slammed Harrison onto the hardwood floor.

The forceful impact with the floor caused Harrison to drop his pistol. He was in shock at the attack but, more importantly, at Gavin's strength.

Straddling Harrison, Gavin began to pummel him in the face with punches.

Harrison did his best to deflect, but Gavin was hitting him repeatedly and fast. He reached for a sheath knife, pulled it, and thrust it deep in Gavin's side.

Gavin wailed in pain but was of a mind to grab Harrison's hand and pull the knife out.

Using his free hand, Harrison clenched it into a fist and drove it into the side of Gavin's face, knocking him off him.

Gavin scrambled to his feet but quickly fell back to the ground after slipping in his own blood.

Feeling he now had the advantage, Harrison got up, knife still in his right hand, and lunged at Gavin.

Gavin dodged the advance by leaping away. He started to crawl but was stopped when Harrison jumped on his back. Fear gripped Gavin, he was losing, and this loss would equal his death. He looked up and saw a beating hammer used for binding. It had a heavy four-pound flat head and a sturdy wooden handle. He extended as far as he could and grabbed it, then spun around. Using every ounce of strength in his body, he swung it hard, slamming the head of the hammer into the side of Harrison's head.

Harrison fell to the floor and flopped around.

Not wanting to give Harrison a chance to get back up, Gavin jumped on him and slammed the hammer several more times into his head until he stopped moving.

Tired and exhaling heavily, Gavin dropped the bloody hammer and fell to the floor. He was exhausted and had lost a lot of blood.

"Gavin, are you okay?" Elmer asked, shifting around on the floor to get a better view of Gavin.

"No, I'm not okay," Gavin said, feeling a heavy fatigue wash over him.

"Stay awake, you hear me," Elmer said.

Gavin was so weak he couldn't reply. He closed his eyes and drifted off.

ELSTON, MISSOURI

The governor's patience and desire had reached its peak.

He wanted to see what he'd paid so much to have. He marched up the stairs, down the hall, and was now standing in front of the red room door.

Baron had escorted him up, but remained quiet, knowing the governor was preparing himself mentally.

"They're in here?" Strauss asked.

"Yes, here's the key. Unlock it and go inside," Baron said, opening his hand to reveal a skeleton key.

Strauss took the key, but before he inserted it into the lock, he said, "You can go."

"Would you like me to send up anyone to be outside the door?" Baron asked.

"No, I want my privacy," Strauss replied.

"When you're finished, please come down and join the party. It will start in a couple of hours," Baron said, giving a nod then turning and briskly walking away.

Strauss waited for Baron to disappear from sight before he inserted the key. When he did, he turned and unlatched it. Grabbing the knob, he turned it slowly and pushed the door open.

On the bed sat a terrified Emma and a determined-looking Anna, her right hand behind her back.

He stepped into the room and closed the door, ensuring to lock it.

A lone candle lit the room, but enough light was creeping in through the slits in the window to provide him adequate light to see.

He took a couple of steps, set the key on a small table, and said, "Hello, girls."

Neither girl uttered a word.

"Do you remember me? I'm a friend of your father's. I'm Governor Strauss; I run this state," he said as if bragging about his position would be alluring to the girls. He was nervous and it showed in his tone. He took a few more steps closer.

Emma tensed while Anna remained as she was when he first came into the room.

"You're both so quiet," he purred.

A tear broke from Emma's right eye and streamed down her cheek.

"Don't cry. There's nothing to be afraid of," he said, drawing closer to Emma.

His ever-encroaching presence horrified Emma, who grasped Anna's knee and squeezed.

Anna didn't feel Emma's grip. She had pushed all the pain out of her body and focused solely on what she had to do.

A second tear came to Emma's eye.

Strauss reached to wipe it off.

Emma recoiled.

"Don't fear me. I won't hurt you," he said softly.

Emma's entire body began to tremble.

"You're so frightened. Come, let me hold you," Strauss said, reaching out with both arms to embrace Emma.

Anna saw her moment. With the glass shard in her hand, she lashed out, striking Strauss with one perfect strike into the side of his neck.

He stood up and placed his hand over the wound. "What have you done?"

Anna came at him with a fury, stabbing him repeatedly in the torso. She battered him with a relentless barrage until he toppled to the floor. She climbed onto him and kept plunging the glass deep into him.

He tried to fight back, but the surprise attack was too much. He gagged on his own blood and quickly died.

Anna didn't stop. She kept stabbing him over and over, tears bursting from her eyes.

Emma came to her and said, "Enough."

Anna froze, the shard high over her head, ready to take another stab.

"He's dead," Emma said, gently touching Anna, afraid of the girl she had just witnessed ferociously attacking Strauss, yet sympathetic and grateful.

Anna looked up, her face covered in streaks of blood. "Come, we must go."

The two girls grabbed the key, unlocked the door, and ran into the hallway. Seeing it was clear, they headed left, hoping it would take them to an exit.

***

Abigail reached the outskirts of the plantation. She dismounted the horse and swatted it away. She knew she couldn't just go riding in guns blazing. She was no doubt outnumbered, outgunned, and was in an unfamiliar territory. She'd have to conduct this with stealth and quick decisive brutality. In other words, kill everyone, but do it quietly.

Her side was throbbing from the hard ride, but she

didn't have any other choice but to accept it.

With the Ithaca slid into a scabbard strapped to her back, the tomahawk in her belt, and her trusty Colt on her side, she ran down the edge of the road until she came to a large wrought-iron fence that encircled the estate house. There she had a good vantage point to evaluate how many people were outside as well as how she could best access the house unseen.

At the front gate she saw two men, both armed with rifles. At the front double door one man stood; he appeared to be unarmed. Other than that, she didn't see anyone. She made her way along the fence until she could see a back entrance, to find it was unmanned. This would be her way in. She pulled the tomahawk from her belt and held it in her hand firmly. She took a deep breath, exhaled, and slipped between the rails of the fence then took off for the back door. She reached it in a manner of seconds. When she went to see if it was unlocked, the door opened. Quickly she pressed her back to the side of the cold brick house.

A woman wearing an apron stepped out, holding a large woven basket.

After the woman closed the door, Abigail nabbed her. She brought her close, her hand covering her mouth, and with the sharp edge of the tomahawk against her throat, she asked quietly, "Where are the girls?"

The woman gasped and mumbled something unintelligible.

"I'm going to remove my hand. You scream, I'll cut your throat. Nod if you understand."

The woman nodded.

Slowly Abigail removed her hand. "Where are the girls?"

"Which ones?"

"How many are here?"

"Six."

"They're all upstairs, second floor?" Abigail asked.

"Yes, east hall." The woman groaned in fear.

"How many people inside?" Abigail asked.

"I don't know."

Abigail pressed the edge of the tomahawk hard against her neck, drawing blood. "How many?"

"One, two, three, six," the woman said as she counted out loud. "There's six inside, yes, six."

"Six and you make seven? Does that include the men out front?"

"Seven including me, and there are three out front and one in the barn," the woman said.

Abigail had all the information she needed. It wasn't as bad as she imagined. Knowing some of those six inside were Baron and staff, she estimated one, maybe two were guards. She then found herself curious as to what the woman did there. "What's your purpose here?"

"It's not my fault," she cried.

"What's your purpose here?" Abigail repeated.

"I get them ready for the clients," the woman answered.

Abigail's anger welled up. There was no excuse this woman could give for what she did.

"That's all, it's not my fault," the woman cried.

Unable to control her anger, Abigail slit the woman's throat. "Not a good answer." She dragged the woman and dumped her behind a large shrub. "One down, ten more to go."

***

Anna and Emma came to the end of the hallway but found it dead-ended. They quickly turned around and sprinted back.

"What about the others?" Emma asked.

"We can't worry about them," Anna said.

Emma stopped. "No, we must help them too."

"What? No, we can't risk it," Anna said, taking Emma's hand and pulling her.

"I have the key. I'm letting them out," Emma said, walking to the nearest door and opening it. Inside they found Evelyn, the girl they had first met on the train.

"Emma, Anna?" Evelyn asked, surprised to see them.

Emma waved and said, "Come on, we're getting out of here."

Evelyn didn't hesitate; she jumped from the bed, her bright white dress flowing as she ran. "Where are we going?"

"Anywhere but here," Anna said.

They went to each door and freed the other children.

With all of them now free, six in total including Anna and Emma, they made for the stairwell at the end of the hall.

When they reached it, they ran right into Devon, who was alarmed to see them all.

"You're out? What's going on?" Devon bellowed. He turned to warn the others but not before Anna came down on him with the shard, stabbing him repeatedly with the glass.

Devon managed to toss her off, but his wounds were catastrophic. He toppled down the stairs, only stopping when his body reached the ground floor with a loud thud.

The girls picked Anna up and raced down the stairs but were forced to retreat back up when a servant came to Devon's aid and looked up to see them. "Baron, they're out!"

Back on the second floor, the girls huddled, with Anna taking charge. "We need to hide. We'll do so in one room; we'll barricade ourselves in."

"Are you sure?" Ashley asked. She was the twelve-year-old from the train.

"We don't have a choice. It's fight or now possibly die," Anna said.

Showing a new strength, Emma declared, "Girls, we're fighting back."

They all nodded and followed Emma down to the last room in the hall and slammed the door closed behind them.

Emma locked it while the others began to stack up furniture against it.

Down below, Baron came sprinting from the parlor. When he saw Devon's dead body on the floor encircled in blood, he roared with anger. "Guards, everyone, get those girls."

Outside, Abigail heard the commotion. She wasn't sure if it had to do with her; either way, the time was now. She entered the house and stepped into a short and narrow hallway. Quickly she passed through, coming to a door. She opened it and peeked out to see a body at the bottom of a narrow stairwell. Twenty feet past that was a grand staircase that came off the large foyer.

The three men from the front poured in through the front doors and ran up the grand staircase. While a couple of others, including a short fat man, ran up the other stairs.

With the ground floor looking clear, Abigail entered and ran to the narrow set of stairs.

"Who are you?" a man shouted at Abigail.

She turned and saw a man dressed in a tuxedo. By all appearances he appeared to be a servant. He was unarmed, but to Abigail that didn't matter. She cocked her arm back and threw the tomahawk as hard as she could. It tumbled through the air, making three revolutions before impaling the man in the chest.

He dropped to his knees and fell over.

Abigail ran, pulled it out, and headed up the narrow stairs, where she heard a lot of hollering. Just before cresting the top stair, she put the tomahawk away, removed the shotgun and cocked both hammers. She peeked around the corner and saw a gaggle of men, totaling five, beating and hammering on a door at the end of the hall.

"Open this door at once!" Baron screamed, his fat

face beet red.

Inside, the girls had gathered in the corner, all holding something they hoped they could use to protect themselves if the men managed to get inside the room.

Abigail stepped into the hallway. She locked eyes with the men and began to march down the hall.

Out of the corner of his eye, Baron saw the movement. He turned and saw Abigail. "Men, stop her!"

Two of his guards swiveled, rifles in their hands.

Abigail already had the shotgun firmly in the pocket of her shoulder. She aimed and pulled one trigger. The double-aught buck struck the first man. She quickly took aim on the other and pulled the trigger, striking him with the shot.

Both men cried out in pain, dropped their weapons, and folded over.

Inside the room, the girls cried out when they heard the gunfire.

Abigail broke the breach of the shotgun, loaded two shells and closed it. She cocked the hammers and raised it but not before a guard shot her in the leg, the bullet passing just through the fleshy part. She stumbled, got her footing, took aim on him, and pulled the trigger on both barrels, blasting him with twice the amount of shot as the others.

The force of the blast sent the man flying through the air.

She was now ten feet away from the two remaining men, Baron and a servant.

Baron reached for a rifle.

Abigail didn't have time to reload. She threw the shotgun at him, striking him in the arm.

Baron dropped the rifle.

She pulled her Colt and fanned the hammer twice, shooting the servant. She cocked it again and walked up to Baron. "Are you Baron?"

"You're that bitch bounty hunter," he spat, cowering like a child against the door.

"My name is Abby Sure Shot, and I'm here to kill you."

"Take the girls, take them, but don't hurt me," he begged.

"I'm taking the girls and killing you," she said, pulling the trigger.

The girls heard the chatter outside and the final shot.

Anna thought she recognized the voice and cried out, "Is that you, Abigail?"

Hearing Anna, Abigail replied, "It's me, Anna. Let's get you and the others out of here."

JEFFERSON CITY, MISSOURI

Abigail was able to control the bleeding from the flesh wound on her leg and get all the girls back to the rectory safely using a wagon from Baron's stable and the cover of night for concealment.

When she arrived, she was surprised to find Aiden at the door, covered in blood.

"You're alive, thank the heavenly Father," Aiden said, looking up as if praying.

"Are you okay?" she asked, motioning to his blood-covered shirt.

"The blood isn't mine, it's Gavin's. He's been injured badly," Aidan said, opening the door wide. Only then did he see all the girls behind Abigail. "Look at you, girls. Come inside, please come in. This is a sanctuary for you."

Abigail turned to the girls and said, "It's fine. He's a good man, not like the others. This is a safe place."

One by one the girls entered the house, each finding a place to sit.

The last one was Anna.

Aiden just stared at her, horrified that she was covered in blood from her head to her feet.

"Sweetheart, come with me. Let's get you cleaned up," Abigail said, taking her hand and limping across the threshold.

"You're hurt?" Aidan asked Abigail after noticing the limp.

"Father, these days, I feel like I'm always hurt," Abigail joked.

"Finn would help, but he's asleep. He was exhausted after taking care of Gavin. Please come into the kitchen and let me take a look at you," Aiden said, leading Abigail and Anna there.

Anna took a seat in a chair while Abigail leaned against the table. "Father, I was hit in the leg. It crazed me, but it stings like a son of a bitch…oops, sorry for cursing."

"It's fine. The Lord forgives you," Aiden said, bringing a bowl of hot water and placing it on the table.

As Abigail slowly removed all of her gear, placing it gently on the table, she asked, "What happened to Gavin?"

"All I got from him was that he was attacked. His employer brought him to us, said that Gavin kept asking for us. He said a man came in, took them hostage, and demanded to see Gavin. When Gavin returned to the shop, the man took him and questioned him about you."

"This man was looking for me?" Abigail asked, curious if it was Harrison. "Any description of the man?"

"No."

"What happened to him?" Abigail asked.

"Gavin killed him," Aiden replied and paused before he said, "I can't clean and bandage your wound with your trousers still on."

Obliging him and showing she didn't have a concern for modesty, she removed her trousers and tossed them on the floor.

Anna watched her with fascination.

Aiden squatted down and said, "Best you sit down."

Abigail did as he requested, grimacing as she went.

"How's your side?" he asked.

"Hurts."

"Anything else?" he asked.

"Like I said, Father, I'm in a constant state of pain these days," she replied.

Using a washcloth, he cleaned the leg wound of the blood so he could better see the issue. "Looks like a graze. You're lucky, a few inches farther into your leg, the bullet could have hit an artery and you would have bled out."

"Count me lucky, then," she said, smiling. Abigail glanced at Anna and gave her a big grin. She was so happy to have succeeded in rescuing the girls and putting down Baron and his cohorts.

"Abby," Anna said.

"Yes."

"I killed two men," she said.

Aiden stopped what he was doing and looked at Anna.

Abigail reached out and touched her face. "It's okay. You did what you had to do. When I'm done here and after you get cleaned up, we'll talk about it."

Anna nodded.

"We can pray about it later," Aiden said.

"It's okay. I'll just talk with Abigail later about it," Anna said, not quite trusting Aiden simply because she'd just met him.

Aiden finished cleaning the wound and bandaged it. He inspected her other bandage and decided to replace it with a fresh one, then turned his attention to Anna. When he started to wipe the blood from her face and arms, he said, "How about you remove the dress?"

She shook her head.

"She's going to need a little time, Father," Abigail said. "How about you leave us and I'll finish up in here."

Aiden nodded and left the room but not before gathering a plate of food for the other girls to eat.

Alone, Abigail said, "He's right, let's get that filthy dress off."

Anna removed it, letting it fall to the floor.

"I'll get it washed," Abigail said.

"Throw it away. I don't ever want to see it again," Anna spat.

Abigail gathered the dress and looked at it. She understood why Anna was repulsed by it and tossed it in a basket of garbage. When she put her eyes on Anna's battered body, she could only think of herself and that this girl didn't look much different than herself. "How does your shoulder feel?"

"Sore."

"And here?" Abigail asked, pointing at her gunshot wound.

"Same," Anna said.

"I'll tell you what, I'm going to clean you up and change those bandages," Abigail said, wringing out a warm clean washcloth.

Anna nodded.

Tenderly, Abigail washed her and replaced the old bandages. When she was done, she found her something to wear, and the two sat drinking a cup of tea.

Looking up through the steam of the tea, Anna said, "Why did you come back? I know my parents are dead, so you didn't have to."

"Because it was the right thing to do," Abigail said.

"What will become of my sister and me?" Anna asked, her tone sad.

"Do you have an uncle or aunt, some sort of family?"

"My father's brother lives in Omaha and is married,

no children yet. He works for the railroad," Anna replied.

"Do you want to go live with them?" Abigail asked.

"I suppose, they're nice enough," Anna answered, hanging her head low.

Picking up on her change of state, Abigail asked, "What's wrong?"

"I was hoping we could stay with you," Anna replied, lifting her head and looking at Abigail. The single candle flickered, making their shadows dance on the table and wall.

"Me? Oh, I don't think that would be a good idea. I'm gone all the time, and I couldn't even take care of…" Abigail said before pausing.

"Take care of who? Do you have children?" Anna asked.

"Me, no. No children. I did save a girl by the name of Madeleine from an abusive family. We sort of lived together, but it didn't work out, so she now lives with this nice family in Dallas. They have a big farm with animals, dairy cows and such. It was for the best."

"Did Madeleine want to go live with this family?"

All Abigail could think was, *Here we go again.* In a matter of days someone else was asking her about Madeleine. She thought about the question, hesitating only because she knew her answer would only prompt another question and so forth.

"You don't have to talk about it," Anna said, giving Abigail a way out.

"No… I mean, no, I want to talk about it with you; I'm just thinking how to best answer it…I suppose she didn't want to live there thinking they were her full-time parents. She wanted me to be her mother, but I just couldn't be. This might sound horrible, but in order for me to always be around, I need to give up what I do, but I can't, I won't. I like what I do."

"Did she tell you to give up what you do?"

Abigail thought and said, "No."

"Did she tell you that you always needed to be there?"

"Not directly, she would just get sad and tell me to stay longer when I was leaving," Abigail answered.

"That's what all people say when someone we love has to go, but we understand why they need to go."

"I suppose you're right."

"How did she take it when you said it wasn't going to work out?" Anna asked.

Abigail chuckled and said, "You're full of questions."

"I'm just trying to understand adults. They say they love someone then hurt them."

Anna's comment gave Abigail pause. She stewed on it then said, "It's complicated sometimes."

"Why does it have to be complicated? If you want to see her and spend time with her when you can, why can't you do that? Why does it have to be one way or the other?"

"You're right again."

"What's that old saying, from the mouth of babes," Anna said, smiling.

"Can we change topics and talk about what happened?" Abigail asked.

Anna looked down and asked, "Are you referring to me killing the governor?"

Shocked by what she said, Abigail asked, "The governor, what governor?"

"Governor Strauss was the person who had us taken. He was there last night. I killed him when he came into the room with me and Emma," Anna confessed.

"You killed the governor of Missouri?" Abigail asked, truly flabbergasted by Anna's confession.

"Yes, I stabbed him, like, thirty times," Anna answered.

Abigail stood up abruptly and said, "We need to go."

"Go where?" Anna asked, looking at Abigail with concerned eyes.

"Anywhere that's not Missouri," Abigail said, leaving the kitchen to go find Aiden.

In the front room, Aiden was reading to the girls. He looked up from the book and smiled.

"Can we talk?" Abigail asked.

"Sure," Aiden said, putting the book down.

"In private?" Abigail asked as she headed for the front door of the rectory.

"Oh, yes," Aiden said, following her out. He closed the door behind them and asked, "What's the matter? You look startled."

"I need to get Anna and Emma out of the state now, like this morning," Abigail said.

"What's wrong?" Aiden asked, folding his arms and growing tense.

"Anna killed Governor Strauss last night. He was the

key individual behind this entire thing. He was there and she put an end to him."

Aiden made the sign of the cross and closed his eyes in prayer.

"We need to leave. I'll need you and Father Leary to care for and find the others homes," Abigail said.

Aiden stopped praying and said, "We can do that."

"There's no time to waste," Abigail said.

"Where will you go?" Aiden asked.

"To Omaha, they have an uncle there," Abigail replied.

"I'll go gather some things for your trip," Aiden said then went back inside the house, followed by Abigail.

Inside, Abigail found Anna now in the front room sitting next to Emma.

"Girls, we're going to leave," Abigail said.

"Where are we going?" Emma asked.

"To your uncle's place in Omaha," Abigail answered.

Emma gave Anna a look of concern.

"It will be fine, Emma. Uncle James is a nice man; he's father's brother, if you remember," Anna said.

Anna and Emma hadn't seen Uncle James in years, as he had spent a considerable amount of time traveling the world only to recently return with a wife from Europe. He settled in Omaha after taking a position from his brother on the railroad.

"Is everything alright with that?" Abigail asked.

"It's just that we don't know him that well. We'll be fine there," Anna replied.

"Good, go help Father Harris. He's giving us some

provisions for the trip."

"Miss Abigail?" Emma asked, still sitting pensively on the couch.

"Yes."

"What about Mother and Father? Where are they?" Emma asked, referring to the location of their bodies.

Abigail hadn't thought about them since she'd heard about their murder. "I'll make arrangements to have their remains sent to Omaha once we arrive there."

"And what about our things in Topeka?" she asked.

"It will all be fine, Emma. I'm sure Uncle James will have them brought to us in Omaha," Anna said.

A growing fear was rising in Abigail. She knew it was only a matter of time before the law arrived at Baron's estate and saw the carnage and found the governor's body.

Aiden stepped out of the kitchen, holding a basket, and said, "I packed food for several days."

Abigail limped over and took it. "Oh, before I forget, that tomahawk came in handy," she said. "It's on the table in the kitchen."

"Take it with you. Father Leary and I received it—" Aiden said but was cut off.

"He told me the story and, no, I don't think I can take it," she said.

"No, please, I'll go get it for you," Aiden said, going back into the kitchen. He came out with it in his hands. He gave it to her and said, "It belongs with you now."

"I'd go say goodbye to Gavin and Father Leary, but I don't want to disturb them. Tell them both I appreciate their help," Abigail said.

"Can I give you a hug?" Aidan asked Abigail.

"Of course, just don't squeeze too hard," Abigail said.

The two embraced.

"Is there anything else I can do for you?" Aiden asked.

"You've done so much, but I do have a few things that I need done. I don't know what happened to Mr. Fisk, he was a reporter who was with us then disappeared. I fear the worst, but if you see him, let him know that I'll be in touch. I also need you to remove Dwight's body from that bar display and have him buried. I'd do it myself, but I'm in a hurry. Plus if I went up there, I assure you there'd be more bodies after I left. And finally this, can you send this telegram for me?" she said, handing him a folded piece of paper.

Aiden took it and read the short note. A smile creased his face. "You're going to see her, that's nice. Finn mentioned her. I'm happy for you; and this telegram will make a little girl in Dallas very happy."

"Take care, Father," Abigail said.

"Goodbye, Abigail, may God ride with you," he said.

Abigail disappeared into the dark of night. She climbed onto the wagon, turned to the girls, and asked, "Are you ready?"

"Let's go. I never want to see this place again," Anna said.

CHAPTER EIGHT

CHICAGO, ILLINOIS

APRIL 17, 1891

Upon hearing he was being summoned to the president of the company's office, Gillian ensured he looked his best. It wasn't every day he was called up to the twentieth floor, so if he was going to go, he'd make sure he made an impression.

He briskly walked to the door and stopped short of knocking.

The top section of the door was frosted glass, and emblazoned on it was the name of the occupant, Gerald O'Hare, President.

Gillian cleared his throat, smoothed his slicked-back hair, and knocked.

"Come in," O'Hare barked.

Gillian opened the door to find O'Hare busy writing at his beautiful mahogany desk, which he had perfectly centered in the room. The office was twice as large as his with a view that was comparable.

"Mr. Gillian, stop lollygagging. Come in and take a seat; make sure you close the door behind you," O'Hare barked.

"Yes, sir," Gillian said, closing the door and promptly taking a seat.

An awkward minute passed with O'Hare sitting, still

writing, and Gillian nervously looking around the room, waiting for his boss to say something.

O'Hare put his pen down and stared at the paper. He nodded, folded it up, and placed it in the top drawer. Upon closing the drawer, he looked up at Gillian and said, "The Fulton case."

"Yes, sir, I was just about to send a couple more men down there to investigate what happened to our men," Gillian happily said, feeling that he was adequately handling the case.

"No one else is to go to Jefferson City. The case is closed," O'Hare said.

Gillian's content expression gave way to confusion. "I don't understand."

"What's not to understand? The case is officially closed. We mourn those two men, and we're preparing to receive their remains any day now. Once they go into the ground, we can put this entire mess behind us."

"Sir, we don't let a case go unsolved, especially one where we've lost two of our own. We don't know what happened and are attempting to find out. I have a lineup of interviews to do, one being that bounty hunter Abby Sure Shot."

"I don't give a damn about any interviewee, and I especially don't give a damn about this Abby Sure Shot or whatever she calls herself. The case is closed, period."

"So that's it? These two men's deaths go unsolved? What about the morale of our employees?" Gillian said.

"I expect you to handle the morale, and if anyone has issues with my decision in regards to this case, they can go work somewhere else," O'Hare barked.

Gillian was perplexed as to why the case was being closed, but he would do what he was told. He'd worked too hard and for far too long to jeopardize his position with the company. "I will do what you say, sir. The Fulton case is hereby closed."

"Good, now you can go," O'Hare said, reaching for an envelope that was clearly marked as a sealed telegram.

Gillian got up; his legs felt wobbly; he'd let his nerves affect his physical well-being.

O'Hare glanced up and asked, "Why you still standing there?"

"On my way out," Gillian said and hurried out the door. After closing it, he sighed loudly. He didn't know what to make of his encounter. It was the opposite of what he thought it would be. He proceeded to his office, closed the door, and fell into his chair. In the center of his desk sat the Fulton case file. He opened it up, thumbed through a few notes, then closed it. Opening his top drawer, he pulled out a rubber stamp, dabbed it on an ink pad, then pressed it on the folder cover. He removed it and stared. It read CASE CLOSED. Using his pen, he signed and dated it. He did wonder why the case needed to be closed without understanding what had happened to both Milton and Harrison. He shook his head, dismissing all his own beleaguered questions, placed the file in a cabinet, and never saw it again.

JEFFERSON CITY, MISSOURI

Aiden heard the knock on the front door. "I'll get it," he called out, walking from the kitchen. He opened the door to find two strangers. "Hello, how may I help you?"

"My name is Langdon, and this is my wife, Matilda. We're Gavin's parents."

"Why, yes, please do come in," Aiden said, opening the door fully.

Langdon and Matilda entered and stood just inside. Both looked out of place as if in a foreign world where no one looked or spoke anything familiar.

"Can I take your coat and hat?" Aiden asked Langdon.

"Sure, thank you," Langdon said, handing them to Aiden.

Finnegan emerged from the hallway and said, "Let me guess, you're Gavin's parents?"

Both nodded.

"How is he?" Matilda asked, a look of deep concern written all over her face.

"He's doing very well. No infection, and today was the first day he woke with an appetite. I was just going to the kitchen to get him something to eat," Finnegan said.

"May I see him?" Matilda asked.

"Of course, where are my manners," Aiden said, motioning for them to follow him.

They went to the bedroom where Gavin was recuperating and entered.

Gavin was sitting up, several pillows behind his head

and a book in his lap. He looked and first saw Matilda. "Mother," he cried out, closing the book.

She rushed to him and gave him a warm embrace.

"Don't squeeze too tight," he said, laughing.

Matilda peppered him with kisses all over his face. "My dear beautiful boy, I've been so worried about you."

"I've missed you too," he said, still laughing.

"What happened?" she asked.

"He's a hero is what he is," Aiden said with a smile.

"Hero?" Langdon asked, shocked to hear those words associated with Gavin.

"Yes, he stood his ground against a very evil man and helped save a group of girls who had been kidnapped."

"He helped save…wait, my Gavin fought and saved people?" Langdon asked, his jaw hanging open.

"Yes," Finnegan said, coming into the room with a tray. He placed it on the nightstand and continued, "The last of the girls left this morning. If it weren't for him, things may not have turned out well. Your son is a very brave man."

Gavin glanced at Langdon, who stood near the door looking as nervous as he'd ever seen him.

Langdon returned the look with eyes full of pride.

"I didn't know you'd come," Gavin said to Langdon. "When I had Father Leary send the telegram, I just wasn't sure."

"Of course we'd come," Matilda said.

Langdon stepped forward, his eyes moist. "Son, I have something to say."

Aiden and Finnegan gave each other a look then got up and left the room so Gavin and his parents could have privacy. Outside the room, Finnegan said, "Good work, Father Harris."

Aiden smiled and said, "Good work, Father Leary."

Wanting what he had to say to be an intimate moment, Langdon closed the door and came to the bedside. He looked down and said, "Gavin, I am deeply ashamed of my behavior that night. Will you forgive me?"

Gavin took his hand and squeezed. "I forgive you, but can you forgive me? I left you when you said you needed me. I was selfish, and now I'm lying here nursing a stab wound."

"You're lying there because you have become the total embodiment of everything I could have wanted for you; you're a man, more than I am. All a father can ever want of his son is to be better than he was, a good, moral and upstanding gentleman, strong in body, mind and spirit, and you're all that. I am so sorry I ever doubted that." Tears started to fall from his eyes.

"Thank you for saying that," Gavin said.

"What happened?" Langdon asked. "Give me all the details, specifically about your encounter with this evil man you slayed."

"Langdon, we're not going to have him tell stories. He needs to rest. Maybe later, when he's well enough to get up from this bed."

"How about I tell you when I come home with you?" Gavin said.

"Come home with us?" Langdon asked, looking

surprised by the comment.

"I want to come home. I want to work on the farm, where it's peaceful and, I will admit, fulfilling. I've learned many things on this brief adventure of mine, and one is we take our lives for granted. It wasn't until I was gone did I truly appreciate what you and Mother have done for me. How wonderful and special a life you've created for me. I might leave again in the future to go work somewhere else, but for now, I want to be with my family."

"I've not heard better words in my life," Langdon cried.

Matilda took Gavin's other hand and kissed it. "And when that day comes that you need to move on, you'll have our support."

"You will. You're a man and you get to decide your own future," Langdon declared.

Gavin smiled; tears came to his eyes as well. He didn't know what was in store for him in the years to come or whether he'd ever leave the farm to find other work. He thought it best to just think about that when it came to him and enjoy what was in front of him now.

OMAHA, NEBRASKA

Abigail packed the last remaining item into her bag and cinched it up. She walked to the window and looked out onto the busy street.

James and his wife lived in a three-story walk-up in downtown Omaha. He was never one who needed much, so the house suited him, as compared to his brother, Edward, who always wanted the biggest house he could afford.

The trip from Jefferson City was uneventful, and for that, she was grateful. While she was clearly able to handle herself, she could use more than a few days not engaged in fighting or gun wielding.

James and his wife, Enid, welcomed the girls with open arms and swore they'd raise them as Edward and Clara would have wanted. This gave Abigail peace of mind knowing the girls would be surrounded by love and nurturing and also meant her job was now officially over.

James' generosity and connections allowed her to have luxury accommodations for her train ride to Dallas. It would take three days and several connections, but soon she'd have Madeleine in her arms.

Laughter echoed from the ground floor, tearing her away from her thoughts. She pulled out her pocket watch and saw it was time to leave. She grabbed her bags and headed downstairs to find Anna and Emma playing; she watched them for a brief moment, mesmerized by their innocent playfulness. So odd that they could now play like this after having experienced so much horror.

On the trip from Jefferson City, she had spoken with Anna at greater depth about the men she had killed. Using her Uncle Billy's words almost verbatim, she had tried to convey the difference between murder and killing, and that what she had done wasn't wrong, and that fighting back and using lethal force in the defense of your own life and the lives of others was justified. Surprisingly,

Anna seemed content and at peace with what she'd done; she had come to this realization all on her own. Not wanting to beleaguer the point, Abigail left it alone.

Upon arriving, she had told James what had happened and to be on the lookout for any telltale signs of stress-related issues concerning the girls' experiences. James pledged to do whatever he needed to do so they would cope and have healthy and fulfilled lives.

"We're going to miss you being here," James said as he walked out of his parlor, a big smile on his face. "It's not every day we are graced with a celebrity."

"I'm not so sure about being labeled a celebrity," Abigail said, her cheeks slightly blushing.

"Ever since you arrived, I have read what I could about you and your exploits. They're really entertaining. Have you thought about writing a book?" James asked.

"No," Abigail replied.

Anna stepped up to Abigail and gave her a big smile.

"And how are you?" Abigail asked.

"Good," she said, reaching out and touching the back strap of Abigail's Colt. "It's very pretty."

"She is, isn't she?" Abigail said, pulling it out and twirling it around on her index finger. "My uncle Billy gave it to me for my eighteenth birthday."

"Uncle James, can I have a pistol for my eighteenth birthday?" Anna asked.

"We'll see. How about we first think about your fifteenth birthday coming up soon," James said, patting Anna on the head.

Abigail holstered the pistol and said, "It's time for

me to go."

"I have a carriage parked out front to take you to the station," James said, reaching for her bags. "And let me take those for you."

Abigail pulled back. "Quite all right."

"If you insist, I wouldn't argue with a woman carrying a pistol," he joked.

Abigail knelt and looked deeply into Anna's light-colored eyes. "I want you to write me, tell me how things are going. Same goes for you too, Emma."

"I will, and can you write back?" Anna asked.

"Of course I will," Abigail said.

Anna wrapped her arms around Abigail's neck and squeezed tight. "Thank you."

"Anytime, if you or Emma ever need anything, let me know; same goes for you too," Abigail said, looking at James last.

"Please come visit us if you're ever in Omaha," James said.

"I will," Abigail said, pulling away from Anna and standing. She hated goodbyes and wanted to get this over with. "You all take care of yourselves," she said and headed out the door. She raced down the concrete steps and tossed her bags inside the carriage. Just as she was about to board, Anna cried out, "Wait!" Abigail turned and saw Anna running towards her.

Anna ran into her arms and said, "I saw something at the post office yesterday."

Confused by what she was saying, Abigail asked, "Saw what?"

Anna pulled away, dug into a pocket of her skirt, and pulled out a piece of paper. She unfolded it and handed it to Abigail. "It's him."

Abigail looked at the paper, a wanted poster for a man named Albert.

"It's him, it's the man that took us in Topeka," Anna said, pointing at the sketch of the man.

"Are you sure?" Abigail asked.

"I'm positive. It's him, it's the Albert that took me and Emma," Anna said. "I took it when I saw it. I didn't tell Uncle James, as I don't want him involved. I don't want him to get hurt."

Abigail nodded slightly as her mind began to process how she would find him.

"Train leaves in twenty-five minutes, ma'am," the carriage driver said.

"Anna, I need to go, but thank you for this," Abigail said, folding the wanted poster and sliding it into her vest pocket.

"Please do come visit us. Don't be like other adults who say they'll do something then don't," Anna pleaded.

"I promise I will. I can't guarantee when that will be, but I will," Abigail said, petting Anna's head.

"When I grow up, I want to be just like you. I want to be a bounty hunter," Anna said.

Abigail opened her mouth and was about to give a canned response but stopped short of saying it. Anna was a strong willed and brave girl, not unlike her, so the reality was Anna could do what she did, she could grow up and be just like her. "I'll tell you what, hold that thought, but be flexible too. If there's one thing I'll say, don't let the world dictate what you can be; you do what you want. To hell with the naysayers. Surround yourself with likeminded people who will support you and go out into the world claiming what you want, not what others say you deserve. You hear me?"

Anna nodded.

"Study, learn, absorb as much knowledge as you can get your hands on, and when you turn eighteen and if you still want to be a bounty hunter, you can ride with me," Abigail said.

"You mean that?" Anna asked.

"I do."

"Thank you," Anna said, squeezing Abigail again in a tight embrace.

"I need to go now. My train leaves soon," Abigail said, bending down and giving Anna a kiss on top of the head. "Goodbye, Anna."

Anna let go and stood tall.

Abigail got into the carriage.

As the carriage departed, Anna cried out, "I love you, Abby Sure Shot!"

CHAPTER NINE

DALLAS, TEXAS

APRIL 20, 1891

As the train slowed, Abigail could see the depot ahead and spotted Madeleine right away. When she'd given Aiden the telegram to send, she prayed it would reach Madeleine and that she would be receptive. When she'd sent a second one herself announcing when she'd arrive, she'd hoped upon all hopes that she would be at the station. Seeing her was proof she'd gotten both and, more importantly, that she wanted to see her.

Rarely one to get nervous, she felt a tinge of it wash over her. She didn't know what to expect from Madeleine. Would she express disappointment or anger because of their last conversation, or was all forgiven?

Never in her life had she felt such love for someone; yes, she had loved Uncle Billy and Aunt Nell, and she could even say she felt a kinship towards Grant and Dwight; but how she felt for Madeleine was something entirely different. They say one can only deeply love a child if they come from you, but Abigail disagreed with that notion. She'd do anything for Madeleine, even die for her, so when she had told her the last time that she wouldn't see her again and that it was for her own good, the pain was immense. Knowing she'd never see

Madeleine destroyed her inside, but at that time she felt it was what Madeleine needed, but she'd come to find out how wrong she was.

The job to find the Fulton girls and eventually save all those children, now known as the Lost Ones, had given her something other than the satisfaction of saving a child from the clutches of evil; it had opened her eyes that each and every child needs not only their parents but anyone who can be a direct and positive influence. She knew she wasn't perfect, but with Madeleine's best interests in mind, she would help guide her, and yes, maybe even teach her how to shoot or throw a knife; but more importantly she could be there for her when she needed a shoulder to cry on or a bit of advice. Because we all need people to share the good times and the bad, to know there's support for those days when all seems hopeless.

Abigail didn't wait for the train to come to a full stop. She leapt from the steps, landing on the platform with both feet firmly.

Madeleine squealed and raced towards her. "Abigail, you're here!"

Overwhelmed with emotion, Abigail dropped to her knees, opened her arms, and waited for Madeleine to come.

Madeleine jumped into Abigail's arms.

The two held each other for what felt like an eternity.

"I've missed you so much, Abby. Are you home for a while?" Madeleine asked.

"Yes, I'll be here for a bit; then I'll have to go back

on the trail of another bad man," Abigail replied, thinking her next job had to be hunting down Albert.

She liked hearing Madeleine say home. It had been a while since she had one, and for her Madeleine was definitely that. She'd learned so much on this last job from some of the most unlikely of people. Like her first job with Grant Toomey, this one ended on a bittersweet note. Yes, she'd discovered some things about herself, but she had also lost a trusted confidant and friend, Dwight. She didn't know when she'd find a new partner or if she wanted one. Finding someone like Dwight, a friend and ally she could trust, was difficult, and when they went, they just couldn't be replaced easily.

She stood, Madeleine's hand in hers, and walked to gather her things. She looked down at Madeleine, a grin spread across her tender face, her eyes beaming with joy. It felt so good to be wanted, to be loved. She'd never again allow anything to get in between that.

Every job she went on came with a cost and a reward. Finding the Lost Ones proved to be her toughest and most rewarding of them all. The cost was losing Dwight; the reward was finding her way home.

EPILOGUE

LAWRENCE, KANSAS

MAY 23, 1891

The bartender pulled the bottle back from Albert and barked, “No money, no whiskey.”

“Damn it, I paid you for the first bottle; just put this one on credit. You know I’m good!” Albert fired back.

The outburst silenced everyone else in the smoky backstreet bar.

“Not going to happen. Plus you’re bad luck,” the bartender said.

“Bad luck?” Albert asked.

Putting the bottle back behind the bar, the bartender replied, “Word is anyone you know ends up dead.”

“That’s just coincidence, nothing more, and shouldn’t reflect on my ability to pay my debts,” Albert said.

“It does, ’cause I don’t know if you’ll be around to pay yours,” the bartender said.

“You’re a damn bastard, you know that?” Albert snarled.

“Best you take your leave before I have you removed,” the bartender said.

Albert took two steps backwards and placed his hand on the grip of his pistol.

"Don't be a fool. You might squeeze one off, but friends of mine in here will end you the next second," the bartender growled. He stood drying off a glass, seemingly unconcerned about Albert's threat.

Albert sized up the bartender then slowly glanced around the silent bar. Just to his left he saw four men, hands on the grips of their pistols, ready to pull.

"Albert, go to your boat and get some sleep. Then go find some work so you can pay your tab," the bartender said.

Seeing he was outnumbered, Albert slowly backed away until he was at the front door. "I'll remember this."

"Goodbye, Albert," the bartender hollered.

Albert pushed through the swinging doors and stepped out onto a wood walkway. Before him the street bustled with activity; people darted around from bar to bar; their comings and goings hidden under a moonless night. Lights from a neighboring bar across the street got his attention; he was tempted to try his luck there but changed his mind quickly. Getting humiliated twice in one night was something he wished to avoid. Broke and angry, he headed back to his barge docked on the riverbank of the Kansas River; there he was going to get a good night's rest.

Albert wasn't used to being broke, but after the Fulton case, he found buyers hard to come by, not due to competition but because they were being killed. Weeks after the incidents in Jefferson City, everyone he knew or worked with was being found dead. It unnerved and angered him. He wasn't just scared for his life, he had been left penniless.

He weaved through the streets until he reached the dock. He froze when he spotted a strange light flickering from the aft of his barge. He focused on it for a second before noticing it was the cherry of a cigar. Unsure who it was, he pulled his pistol, cocked it and gingerly walked down the dock until he was feet from the barge. "Who's on my barge?"

"Albert, it's me, Samuel."

"What are you doing on my barge?" Albert asked, holding his pistol out in front of him.

"We need to talk," Samuel said.

"About what?" Albert asked, not moving an inch closer to his barge.

"Albert, are you pointing a pistol at me?" Samuel asked when he noticed Albert's arm raised.

"With everything going on, I can't trust anyone," Albert replied.

"That's why I'm here," Samuel said.

"That's it?" Albert asked.

"Damn it, Albert. How long have we worked together?" Samuel asked.

"A long time but you can't trust anyone. Look what that rat bastard Clay did to you," Albert said, referring to Samuel's driver, Clay, backstabbing him and selling the Fulton girls to someone else.

"He's dead. His body was found dangling in the stocks in Kansas City," Samuel said. "I'm afraid I'll be next."

"What makes you say that?" Albert asked.

"On account that whoever is doing this is systematically killing everyone associated with those girls, from the men Clay sold them to, to Clay. I'm sure to be next, then you," Samuel explained. "Once I saw what was happening, I needed to find you, track you down; maybe we can help each other."

"How?"

"Work together to figure out who's doing it and go get them first," Samuel said.

"You mean hunt them down?"

"Yes."

Albert thought for a second then had an idea. "I don't like this, but I'll help you for a price."

"You're going to charge me?" Samuel asked.

"If you want my help, then yes," Albert confirmed.

"I clearly made a mistake. I thought you'd see the wisdom in it," Samuel said, stepping off the barge and onto the dock.

"You're being paranoid," Albert said, acting as if he didn't have any concerns, which he did.

Samuel walked up to Albert and said, "I also thought we were friends."

"Friends? I never nor do I ever plan on confusing work and pleasure," Albert said.

Samuel shoved Albert aside. "If you change your mind, I'll be at the hotel on State Street," he said then disappeared into the night.

Albert chuckled. He boarded his barge and began to settle in.

He went to turn off his oil lantern when footfalls on

the dock got his attention. "I told you I'm not interested in working together unless you're going to pay me," he hollered.

The footfalls stopped.

"Go away, Samuel," Albert barked.

No reply.

Annoyed, Albert emerged from the cabin and shouted, "Don't be loitering around here. You're not welcome."

The sound of something hurtling through the air gave him pause. He wondered what it was until it smashed into the side of the cabin next to his head. He looked to see it was a tomahawk, its blade half buried in the pine wood. He dove back into the cabin to get his pistol; finding it, he pulled it from the leather and went back out to confront whoever was there, only to walk into the muzzle of a Winchester rifle pointed at his head.

"Drop it," Abigail ordered.

Albert did as he was told, dropping the pistol on the deck. "What do you want?"

"You're Albert, the man who deals in the trafficking of young girls, children," Abigail said, inching closer with her rifle.

"I, um, I think you've made a mistake," Albert said.

Using her left hand, Abigail pulled the wanted poster from her pocket, opened it, and held it up to compare the sketch to Albert. "It's you," she said, tossing the paper at him.

Albert glanced and saw it read *"Alive Only."*

"I'll go peacefully," Albert said.

"We're not going anywhere," Abigail said.

"Will you make a deal? I know where Samuel is; he's a big-name trafficker," Albert said.

"No, I don't make deals with low-down dirty dogs like you," Abigail said.

"But I can lead you to him," Albert said.

"I don't need him," she said.

"If you're the person killing everyone, you'll want him," he said desperately.

"Like I said, I don't need him on account that I already killed him," Abigail declared.

"Not him, but anyone else, I can tell you anything you want to know, anything," he begged.

Abigail lowered the rifle and said, "I need the names of anyone you're with, all of them."

"And if I do, you'll show me mercy?" Albert cried.

Abigail raised her rifle and said, "Names."

"Alright, alright," Albert said. He rattled off a list of names. Many she had already killed. When he was done, he said, "That's it, that's everyone I've ever worked with."

"That's everyone?" she asked, the rifle still pointed at his face.

"Yes, now hold up your part of the deal and let me go," Albert said.

Abigail chuckled. "I never made a deal with you, nor would I ever, 'cause I don't deal with people like you."

"But you said…"

"I never said anything," Abigail said, applying pressure to the trigger. "And everyone you told me, I've already killed them; it appears you're the last one."

"Then take me in. Collect the bounty; don't kill me," Albert pleaded.

"I didn't come here to collect any bounty. I came here to kill you," Abigail said, her finger pulling back more until it discharged. The round struck Albert in the head.

His body slumped over and hit the deck.

She lowered the rifle and stared at Albert's body. It was done. What had started with him had ended with him. She took the oil lantern and smashed it inside the cabin, setting the place ablaze, then stepped off the barge. She cut it free from the dock and shoved it until the now flaming barge was safely away from the dock. She stood and watched it burn until what remained sank beneath the water.

A sense of satisfaction welled up in her. Single-handedly she had killed everyone involved with the abduction of the girls. It wasn't something she had expected to have happen, but each person she had found led to another and another. Her killing spree lasted for three weeks, ending with the one man she had gone to find initially, Albert.

She didn't know what she'd do next, but somehow and for some reason her jobs tended to find her, not the other way around. Knowing this, she decided she'd head back to Dallas and spend time with Madeleine until her next job presented itself.

THE END

THE LOST ONES

ABOUT THE AUTHOR

G. Michael Hopf is the best-selling author of acclaimed series, THE NEW WORLD and other novels. He spent two decades living a life of adventure before he settled down and became a novelist full time. He is a combat veteran of the Marine Corps and a former executive protection agent.

He lives with his family in San Diego, CA

Please feel free to contact him at geoff@gmichaelhopf.com with any questions or comments.

www.gmichaelhopf.com

www.facebook.com/gmichaelhopf

Books by G. MICHAEL HOPF

THE NEW WORLD SERIES

THE END
THE LONG ROAD
SANCTUARY
THE LINE OF DEPARTURE
BLOOD, SWEAT & TEARS
THE RAZOR'S EDGE
THOSE WHO REMAIN

THE NEW WORLD SERIES SPIN OFFS

NEMESIS: INCEPTION
EXIT

THE WANDERER SERIES

VENGEANCE ROAD
BLOOD GOLD
TORN ALLEGIANCE

THE BOUNTY HUNTER SERIES

LAST RIDE
THE LOST ONES
PRAIRIE JUSTICE

ADDITIONAL BOOKS

HOPE (CO-AUTHORED W/ A. AMERICAN)
DAY OF RECKONING
DETOUR: A POST-APOCALYTPIC HORROR STORY
DRIVER 8: A POST-APOCALYPTIC NOVEL

Made in the USA
Las Vegas, NV
05 March 2021

19082935R00142